WHO STIRS THE PORRIDGE IN THE POT?

Who Stirs The Porridge In The Pot

by

Sheila Newberry

Dales Large Print Books
Long Preston, North Yorkshire,
BD23 4ND, England.

British Library Cataloguing in Publication Data.

Newberry, Sheila
    Who stirs the porridge in the pot?

    A catalogue record of this book is
    available from the British Library

    ISBN   978-1-84262-764-8 pbk

First published in Great Britain in 2009

Cover illustration © Jon Browning by arrangement with
Arcangel Images

The moral right of the author has been asserted

Published in Large Print 2010 by arrangement with
Sheila Newberry, care of Judith Murdoch Literary Agency

Dales Large Print is an imprint of Library Magna Books Ltd.

Printed and bound in Great Britain by
T.J. (International) Ltd., Cornwall, PL28 8RW

Acknowledgements

Extracts from articles I wrote for MY WEEKLY in 1985 appear in chapters five and thirteen.
Extracts from my novel THE SUMMER SEASON (Severn House), 2000, appear in chapter fifteen.

Who rises early, brews the tea –
And never has a moment free?
Who gets bathwater piping hot –
Who stirs the porridge in the pot?

Cinderella's Lament
by Betty.

Foreword

I ended my previous memoir, *Seven Pounds of Potatoes Please*, where this story commences.

It was at a low point in our lives, and indeed for the country as a whole: remember the three day week, and rubbish in the streets? For us there was worse to come. However, this trauma, which I shall relate but not dwell on, would actually prove to be the short, sharp shock my husband and I needed to jolt us from despondency.

We moved back to Kent from the West Country, in the late 1970s, after three years running a village shop. We had worked so hard, but it was the wrong time, and place. We had to cut our losses: our priority was a place we could afford which was big enough for a large family. It was a daunting task, but John found what he thought might be a temporary solution.

The family however, were unexpectedly delighted with their new home, a redundant chapel, in a daisy-starred paddock with the village football pitch beyond. The chapel had replaced a primitive structure with a tin roof, which when it rained, drowned out the hymn singing. The foundation stones had been laid by local worthies, and each was inscribed with their name and the date, 1884. Every penny for this construction was raised by public subscription. It must have been a sight to see as it rose, brick by brick over several years of village labour. Recently, with attendance dwindling, the chapel had been sold and suffered rough treatment from speculators, who had abandoned it. We made up our minds to do our best to restore it.

We wouldn't have credited it then, but there were halcyon years ahead, spanning the late Seventies to early Nineties. I have changed a few names but hope to evoke happy memories for those who shared that time and place, and that readers will enjoy these, too.

Return with me to this time and meet again the three lively blond boys, the fifth, sixth and seventh of our nine children, now in their mid-teens, soon to launch themselves in turn to agriculture and engineering, and Katy and Maff, the youngest pair, now eight and six years old.

Our eldest son, J.P., now 21 and settled in Suffolk near my family, recently became engaged to a lovely, auburn haired girl, Di.

Jonathan's sisters, next in line, Sara, Joanna and Virginia, twenty, nineteen and eighteen, have dreams which they are determined to fulfil. Ginge is with us in our new home, completing A levels at high school, but plans to go to teacher training college thereafter. Jo has a good job and social life in London and shares a flat there. Sara is doing well at the college of art. She has already commenced her travelling abroad with sketch books and water colours, when funds allow. They breeze in often at weekends, but they are independent young ladies now.

They all seem to have grown up so fast, one after the other... I guess these 'snapshots' of family life will now focus more on me – hope you don't mind!

One

Who Stirs the Porridge in the Pot?

It was impossible to transform our living quarters overnight, we soon realized it would take us weeks, months, probably years to do so. But our new home in Kent, a mid-Victorian chapel, was a refuge, and once we got to grips with clearing the debris left behind by 'the wreckers' who had ripped out the heart of the place, the family became optimistic over the possibilities. We were helped considerably in our endeavours by the acquisition of an industrial cleaner – a large drum on wheels which could suck up rubble and even water. We needed ear muffs because the whirling drum rattled and crushed the contents and threatened to re-gurgitate them. Fortunately, the chapel walls were thick, so we received no complaints from neighbours.

The children loved all the space; but initially, the only place where I could relax was the cosy former vestry, the one room with doors, where I could shut myself off from the chaos occasionally. I found the illuminated message on the wall of my sanctuary very comforting. It told me: *His Mercy Is Everlasting.*

Rooms were given names, and Katy, when asked to describe her unusual home, by her new teacher, proudly boasted of our 'dog hall.' This was situated beyond a side door to the chapel which was never used, or you would have stepped out on to flattened tombstones. Billow, our Old English cross, had his quarters here, outside the boys' downstairs bathroom, which was designated for their exclusive use because they quickly acquired weekend jobs on local farms, so that area had a pungent smell of manure from their discarded boots.

John placed a notice, *No Boots Past This*

Point! on the door of the little dining room which led to the lofty sitting room. (Some time later I was embarrassed by the sight of one of our young clodhoppers' girlfriends, obediently removing high-heeled, high-fashion boots, before joining us in the other room.)

This vast room was dominated by an enormous chimney breast which John was in the process of building for several years. (It never actually got through the roof.) There was rudimentary central heating, but only the kitchen, the dog hall, two downstairs bedrooms, plus the small living room were cosy in winter. The sleeping bags from our camping days came in handy now, we huddled under these on settees and chairs. I was conscious that visitors, when invited by the young ones, to 'dive under' sometimes wrinkled their noses, because these comforters were not too often in the wash.

That first chill winter we thought we might be warmer up on the gallery, that's if heat really did rise as John often reminded us. He hung a thick sheet of plastic from the beams to hopefully deal with the draughts. The boys obligingly hauled up a settee and armchair and the T.V. We positioned a massive plant pot in a corner to make it look more homely. Unfortunately, one evening we had a visitor. A mouse ventured out from under the eaves and ran up John's trouser leg. The girls screamed and jumped on the settee which rocked and almost went backwards through the plastic screen. John shook his leg, the mouse dropped out and disappeared double quick to more screaming.

John said: 'Why did you make all that fuss? It was my leg, after all.' We moved all the stuff back downstairs again, except for the plant. It thrived up there and almost went through the roof, unlike the chimney.

The boys didn't mind the odd mouse. They turned the gallery into a games area, with Scalextric buzzing at one end. A snooker table was much in use at the other. They didn't worry that the gallery was not railed off. In time, toddling grandchildren sat in safety, in the middle of the green baize. They sometimes left damp patches. Those waiting their turn with the cue fashioned paper aeroplanes and let these flutter down from the gallery on to our heads as we sat below. These paper planes were often minor works of art! The beautiful oriel window cast glorious hues over the floorboards. To one side of the gallery, there was a spare bed, curtained round for visiting friends. We needed to remind them to duck beneath the beam at the top of the stairs; the younger children were happy when they hit their heads on this because it meant they were now taller than five foot! One Swedish visitor said gallantly, 'I had a good night's sleep, I was knocked out and knew no more until morning...' He had also forgotten to dress before finding his way via the vestry dining room to the House of Horrors (the boys' bathroom), but we concentrated on our breakfast porridge and averted our gaze.

John and I, Katy and Maff had bedrooms under the eaves. We had our own bathroom, thank goodness! Even this had its gremlins: we were kept awake for hours one night by what we thought was a drumming session by our neighbours' boys, but eventually twigged it was 'knocking pipes.'

The first two weeks in the chapel, the children were upbeat, liking their new schools, and exploring the surroundings. John and I, however, were suddenly overcome by the enormity of what we had done. We'd returned to familiar territory, it's true, but John had to find a job, and money was dwindling rapidly. I had to 'stir the porridge in the pot' – and scour the saucepan later. John's forte had always been the perfect English breakfast, but we needed to economise. He didn't feel like going out and meeting people, nor did I, but after the three boys and Ginge had left to catch their buses in the morning, it was up to me to walk the two youngest to primary school and later to collect them in the afternoon, for we now lived in a much bigger village and there was a busy road to cross to the school.

We missed the older children a lot. Soon we would be a family of seven, not eleven, I realized, when it was time for Ginge to go to college in Bromley. I blinked back the all too ready tears when I thought of our diminishing numbers.

One afternoon, John was poring over papers spread out on the kitchen table.

'Any letters to post?' I asked hopefully. I had typed out for him a batch of C.V.'s, but we'd had no luck so far.

'No,' he replied, not looking up.

'I'm off to meet the children then...' I wanted to add, 'Would you like to come with me?' but I guessed he wouldn't.

This was a prosperous Wealden village and along the main street on my route, there were distinctive old houses, with newer dwellings in between. On the other side of the road was a discreet small development of family homes built on land which had belonged to the old mill, which sadly, had been dismantled not many years ago. The

23

white boarded mill cottage had a lovely, rioting garden – I wondered who lived there. Someone special, I hoped, because of the history. I would not be disappointed.

I passed the village hall, where so many activities appeared to go on, and came to a quaint little wooden property called *Evergreen*. I half expected to see and hear Jessie Matthews, the musical comedy actress, serenading me over the picket gate. From avid reading of my aunt's pre-war film annuals as a child, I recalled that Miss Matthews had been in a show called *Evergreen* in the Thirties. In the minute front garden, and it was the end of October now, an elderly lady sat facing the street, from a deckchair. She wore a floppy sunhat, a cape and stout boots over thick, ribbed stockings, and she appeared to be snoozing. But the moment I attempted to tiptoe by, her eyes opened wide, and she greeted me, 'Good afternoon,' in clear, ringing tones. She had introduced herself the first day I did the school walk, as 'Miss Bough, pronounced Boff – my friends call me Boffy.' That was the extent of our conversation so far.

Further up the street, set back out of sight, was a manor house in secluded grounds, a dairy farm, the cricket field, and opposite a splendid village green where the bus stopped, a thriving general stores. I had to cross over the road at this point to turn down the church hill. The Saxon church looked out on to a delightful small school. There was the post office stores just before the school, where the waiting mothers congregated. The crossing lady would shortly arrive with her lollipop, to usher them back over the busy road. Most of them would go in the opposite direction to me, past the big shop to the council estate, again a well-thought out extension to the village with excellent housing. This was on the far side of the Green, tucked away behind the church. The mums, some with pushchairs, prams, or with toddlers on reins, glanced at me curiously, as I walked quickly past and down to the school gates. There were two or three mothers already there, ready to collect their children from class one. Matthew was in class two, which was let out ten minutes later. They departed, with a smile and 'hello' to me, then I stood there alone.

The class two children emerged, and scampered up to the shop with pictures in hand, and socks at half mast, to join their parents. I didn't realize then that only the youngest children were supposed to be picked up directly outside the school.

Matthew, the last out, was coming towards me now, dragging his feet. I glanced up as I became aware of a big vehicle arriving outside the shop. A man jumped down from the cab, leaving the engine running, and went inside.

I noticed that it was an oil tanker. Even as I felt Maff slip his hand in mine, I became aware of a voice shouting above the roar of the engine. As if mesmerized, I stared at the tanker, rolling down hill towards us. A woman was waving frantically at me. *'There's no driver!'* she yelled. The other women were frozen to the spot, like me. With them was the driver of the tanker, clutching a packet of cigarettes.

I was suddenly galvanized into action, 'Run!' I cried to Maff, pulling him with me. The ground seemed to come up and hit us as we tumbled over and over.

The next thing I knew the tanker veered and demolished the metal barrier outside the school gates. The engine cut out, and as I struggled up, I saw my little boy lying between the great wheels. I tried to call him, but I couldn't. The mum who had saved us by her quick thinking, arrived, out of breath, but lifted Maff up and dusted him down. 'He's still in one piece, thank God, but he's in shock,' she assured me. There was a helping hand for me, too. The headmaster was holding back the next batch of children, which included Katy, but her teacher, a small, dark-haired Welsh woman, whom I had thought to be strict and not tolerant of fussy parents, couldn't have been kinder. She and my saviour, who I learned had a daughter in Katy's class, took Maff, Katy and me into the school, and Meg, the teacher, my good friend from that day, quickly provided hot, sweet tea. Then she rang John to ask him to collect us. Amazingly, neither Maff or I had sustained any physical damage, though my best coat was muddy and ripped.

The poor Head was in shock, too. He kept saying over and over, 'It's a miracle … it would have been a massacre, if the other children had come out then.'

I really have to end this chapter here. After all these years, it still affects me… I will just add that it came to me too, that it was a miracle. We had been saved despite the odds. Life was worth living after all. I vowed not to feel sorry for myself again.

Two

Happy Days are Here Again

'Hang on a minute,' I said to the children as we were about to go out of the chapel. I dashed upstairs to the bathroom and knocked on the door. It opened, and John stood there looking comical with one side of his face razored-clean and the other side smothered in shaving cream.

'What's up?' he asked, surprised. 'I thought you'd be half way to school by now!'

'I just wanted to say good luck, once more!' I replied, bestowing a kiss on his smooth cheek. I was over the moon with excitement because this morning he had been summoned back for a second interview for a job.

As I rejoined the children, Katy said reproachfully, 'Mum, the White Rabbit's beaten us this morning.' She pointed ahead to a small, hurrying figure, wearing a distinctive white fluffy beret, with a reluctant large child in tow. We couldn't hear what she was saying, but we guessed it would be the same lament as every morning. 'We're late! We *must* be late!' I know it was naughty of me to have thus labelled this harassed mother, but it is a family quirk inherited from my Dad and his family. (His sister, when unexpectedly presented with a sulky young relative, promptly referred to her as 'the impossible child.')

'Last ones this morning,' Cissie the crossing lady said cheerfully. 'Lucky I spotted you coming. The cuckoo's only just gone over.'

'The cuckoo?' I said, then the penny dropped. So, others did this, too, I thought– I wondered what my nickname was... Oh well, whatever it was, I no doubt deserved it.

Cissie paused on the far pavement for a moment. 'It's the W.I. this evening, in the village hall. Seven-thirty. Why don't you come? You'll get to know people then. Mostly the posh lot from the big houses down your way. We could do with a youngster or two to liven 'em up.'

Youngster! I was flattered, being now in my early forties!

'Will you be there?' I asked. Meeting new people was still rather daunting.

''Course I will. Bye then!'

'No, I haven't joined the W.I. yet,' Meg told me, as she shepherded the children into school, having been on the look-out for late comers. 'I'm waiting until I retire! Too many other things to do after school, like marking books, preparing lessons and refereeing netball matches. I wonder if they all turn up in hats still? Mind you, they were jolly good at making all that jam in the war. Millicent plays *Jerusalem* I gather, and dear Mrs Burton does the refreshments, as she does for all the other societies in the village.'

'Is she the lady who rides that big black upright bicycle?' I asked.

'She is indeed. And Millicent is our part-time music teacher. Has Katy a recorder? She'll need one, for the Christmas concert.'

I didn't like to say that after the boys' early-morning practice on the recorder in the past, their father had said he considered it an instrument of torture.

That evening we had two things to celebrate: John felt he'd had an excellent interview, and for some reason the whole family was excited that Mum was going out! My one and only lipstick surfaced from the dressing-up box, the only problem was I didn't have a hat, apart from the woolly pom-pom on top variety for when it snowed. However, Ginge lent me a sparkly hair slide to adorn my hair and I chose court shoes and nylons, rather than the coloured tights and ankle boots I wore as a rule. The village hall was only a hundred yards up the road, and here we had street lighting!

Busy ladies were putting out hard wooden chairs, facing the table for the President, Secretary and Treasurer, which was positioned below the stage. Rather dusty curtains were drawn across this, and Cissie, who had greeted me at the door, whispered: 'We used to put on plays at one time, but not nowadays. We also had a darts team, and played in the local pub, but the new committee disapproved of that.'

The committee didn't look new to me, they were all ladies well over middle age, but at least they didn't wear hats, though some wore silk head scarves to protect their newly set hair. The hairdresser obviously had a busy day when it was W.I. time.

I noted the hatch was up and I could see Mrs Burton counting out the cups on the table and a mouth-watering display of cakes. All for 5p! Mrs B was round, short and rosy-cheeked with bright blue eyes and plenty of laughter lines. I had been informed that she had the prettiest council house garden, that she entered into every aspect of village life with gusto, and was the village wise woman, loved and respected by all.

When it was time for the speaker, and I can't recall a thing about a very dull talk,

Mrs B pulled down the hatch smartly, which showed what she thought of *him*, and not a single W.I. member said a word.

First there was *Jerusalem* and Millicent struck the keys of the piano gamely, while muttering that it needed tuning. She was a handsome woman, with a mass of silvery hair and taught singing as well as piano. I suspected she preferred younger, more enthusiastic pupils, judging by her reproachful sighs at our wavering rendition. Then came The Minutes of the Last Meeting, followed by The Business, which involved every word of every letter or leaflet being read aloud, whether important (or so it seemed to me) or not. The president had a little cough every other paragraph and scanned the audience to see if they were listening. Any Other Business? she enquired, at last. When answer came there none, there was a united soft sigh of relief, until the speaker began shuffling a sheaf of papers.

The Secretary was, to my delight, Miss Bough. She was busy taking notes throughout. When she hadn't nodded off, that is. I would discover that it made absolutely no difference when she read them out next month. There were never any puzzling gaps. Again no-one said a word about her little 'absences' or nudged her awake.

I thought, these quiet, restrained ladies are actually very nice. They respect others' eccentricities, and they obviously care about the Community they live among. They smiled at me, and I smiled back. One of the committee approached me in the break to say, 'What lovely little children you have!' which, naturally made me warm to her. She added: 'I do hope you will want to come again, it's nice to see new faces – and, familiar ones too – Millicent used to provide the music for all our dances here during the war. She worked hard in the land army all day, but she was never too tired to oblige on the piano...'

'And Mrs Burton?' I queried.

'Oh, she was a busy young mother but she could still get twenty cups of tea from a pint of milk and a quarter of tea! She was a wonderful cook even then.'

Millicent, primed by my friend Meg at school, fetched my tea and a large slice of fruit cake. 'This is only my second time,' she confided. 'Cissie said they could do with a bit of insubordination...'

'She hinted at that to me, too,' I said.

'I could hear you singing in the front row,' Millicent told me.

'Oh dear! I know my voice carries – it has to, with so many children to call to attention!' I thought I would make sure I didn't sit in the front seats again, if you twiddled your toes, so to speak, you received reproachful glances from the hierarchy at the table.

'My dear, I intend to find a choir amongst this lot–'

'I don't think I'd be suitable,' I said quickly, before she could suggest I be a part of any singing group.

'Nonsense! You have a good soprano voice,' she said firmly.

Wait 'til I tell the family that, I exulted –
no more requests to 'could you please not
sing so loudly Mum, everyone was looking
at you!' from most of my children in turn,
when I attended a school service.

We were shushed! as the competition was
judged. This was a display of matchboxes,
and the winner was the member who had
managed to pack the most small items in a
Swan Vestas box. I thought this would make
a good game for a rainy day when the young
ones were bored at home.

'The winning box had *six* pins – you can't
get much smaller than that; it's not in the
rules,' Millicent said sotto voce. What rules?
I wondered.

I overheard a couple of other grumbles.
The W.I. were certainly competitive!

I had something else to tell them when I
got home: 'There's a jumble sale on Saturday, and I've been asked to help!'

'We'll all go,' Ginge said. 'So will the girls,
if they're home then.'

'We won't!' cried Dad and the boys.

'Young and able, carry table,' Mrs. Burton winked at me. 'You get away with a lot if you're grey and feeble.' She indicated her own thick grey bob of hair.

I grinned back and unfolded the legs of the trestle. It was quite a tussle. 'You're not feeble,' I told her, 'You set us all an example!'

She tossed me a starched white cloth. 'I've got the best job, overseeing cakes and produce, plus refreshments as usual. Put that large cake to one side. That's for Guess the weight. 10p a go.'

'Glad it's not guess the number of currants,' I joked. 'You don't spare the fruit, it looks yummy! Can I help you on this stall?'

'Sorry, dear, Millicent's asked for you to be with her on the underwear stall – that's very popular, you'll see.'

I didn't fancy that, but I guessed new members drew the short straw.

I cast a regretful glance at my favourite stalls, the bric-a-brac and the books, as I made my way to the end of the hall and a table piled high with mainly white (or sometimes off-white) garments where I was needed to help with the sorting. I knew from past experience that buyers would ignore the neat heaps and dig deep, that garments would land on the floor and be trodden underfoot when the doors opened and the masses rushed in.

Miss Bough was already ready and waiting. She had a small table next to ours for the raffle. She'd sold two books of tickets in advance.

'D'you mind if I have a quick look, dear? I don't suppose I'll get another spare moment until they do the draw...'

Millicent compressed her lips but said nothing. She gave a little shake of her head at me. I chose not to see this. I held up two soft, new vests with sleeves: 'Are these any good to you?' I asked.

'I prefer the Opera top,' Miss Bough said. 'Any nice corsets?'

Millicent couldn't contain herself any longer. 'You must wait until after two o'clock,' she insisted. 'If I find such a garment, I will put it to one side for you.' She gave a slight shudder as she thought about it.

'Thank you, Millicent,' Miss Bough said, sitting down heavily on the chair thoughtfully provided behind her raffle table. She began to rearrange the boxes of chocolates, the writing paper, unwanted gifts like men's sock suspenders, and a solitary bottle of someone's homemade elderberry wine.

The doors burst open and the battle, for it was that, commenced.

It was a chilly day, but underwear wasn't the best-seller of the day. (Although my girls looked pityingly at poor Mum knee deep in chilprufe vests, they patronised the more colourful stalls.) Alas a pair of corsets didn't surface, and there was a growing pile of single socks, but someone nicked (or maybe they paid for) Boffy's stick, which she'd left lying on our table. Fortunately, Chrissie, on the door, recognised it and managed to return it.

The cry went up, 'The gypsies are here!'

However, unlike some of the jumble hunters, who I was assured were not locals, they paid up, even if they struck a hard bargain.

When the crowds thinned out after an hour, I escaped to turn over the books and made two more friends, husband and wife. He was wheelchair bound following an accident on the farm they had proudly taken on as newly weds. I would learn later that Ian had realized a great ambition as a young lad – he had travelled abroad in a banana boat, working as crew, and eventually ended up as a cowboy in the Falkland Islands! It turned out that he was a fellow writer. His wife, Judy, helped with the Brownies and Guides, and illustrated her husband's articles and stories with beautiful pen and ink drawings. Ian had many books to personally recommend. This couple were very involved in village life. They lived in a property behind Miss Bough's.

I went home, weary because 'young and able, collapse and put away table'... All dozen of 'em. Swept up, stacked chairs, sorted the left-overs, oh, it had been fun, but... Still, I had my bargain buy. It hadn't sold on bric-a-brac, but I was offered it for 2p. A tiny statuette of a ballerina, about three inches high. I didn't know it then, but she was art deco. She dances now in our display cabinet. I'd never part with her.

Three

Feathers Flying and Adorning

John was back in the working world, he was now manager of an oil depot. It seemed like poetic justice after the episode of the runaway tanker. The only drawback was that it was a fair old drive away, but he had a company car. This was a great relief to him, to me and the family, but it was coming up to Christmas, and the coffers were still low until the pay cheques rolled in. So, I looked around for a seasonable, reasonable, job. I didn't realize that these two requirements don't always go together.

A notice appeared in the post office window: *Turkey Pluckers Wanted*. Being of a squeamish disposition despite having a large family and having lived for years on a smallholding, I hesitated, then read on. What could be easier or more convenient? The farm was near the school! The hours would tie in very nicely. There would also be a turkey at the end of the stint at 'a special rate' for the workers. That clinched it for me.

I was primed by a regular worker at the farm. 'Wear your oldest clothes, wellington boots and a woolly hat. It's freezing in the plucking shed. You need rubber gloves, a cheese knife and a fine needle and white thread.'

I couldn't imagine what sewing was needed; I have never been a dab hand with a needle, and rubber gloves are cumbersome. Chris had taken over in that department, narrowing all the legs of the boys' jeans, sometimes disastrously, on the sewing machine. They were becoming followers of fashion, with their great Doc Marten boots which took for ever to lace up. (The Pixie Boots were yet to come.) Ginge still sewed beautifully by hand, the patches on her jeans were works of art. She was custodian of the sewing box. She'd provide the right needle.

Cheese knife sounded hopeful, I thought: I visualized a large round cheese on a plate appearing at elevenses, and the workers cutting off a generous slice. I wondered if they supplied nice crusty rolls too...

My informant added: 'A magnet is useful, (She didn't say what for.) She cheered me up with the next statement: 'You get warmed up as time goes on, when the feathers get deep.'

Fortunately, she didn't tell me I'd be a pariah after a couple of days because turkey pluckers had a distinctive smell, or about the possibility of developing tennis elbow. Or about the bout of turkey flu I would no doubt succumb to and have to struggle through. (After the first picking season, the pluckers were mostly immune to this.)

The post office, despite encouraging us with their notice to join the legion of turkey pluckers, now put up a much bigger sign: *No Turkey Pluckers Allowed In This Shop. This doesn't mean just the aliens from other villages, it means YOU*, was unwritten, but I soon realized that this was a fact.

So I joined the boys' boot brigade, but I left mine out in the coal hole as they were even more odorous than our sons' farm boots.

'Turkey plucking – oh dear!' was the opinion of the mums on the school run when they saw my get-up. They couldn't dampen my enthusiasm. That came later, when I was ushered into a dark, draughty shed, where the only light on a dull, grey morning, came through the gaps in the building. The floor was hard-baked mud, there were a few chairs and a large table in the middle. Off this unattractive place (I had visualized a barn with lovely old beams) was another section, from which I could hear the muffled gobbles of turkeys. I nearly turned to make a dash for it, but there was a crowd of us now, jostling for the best seats, away from the worst slits in the wall.

It would be several days later, before any of these experienced workers would deign to speak to me, the interloper. I was given some basic instructions by a Scottish girl which was the only help I received. Jeanie very kindly helped me to fold back the rigid wings of my first turkey, which was the only one I managed during the morning. 'Do those first,' she advised. The cheese knife, I learned was for quilling. You placed your plucked bird on the table and went carefully all over it to remove any remaining quills or stubborn feathers. The needle and thread was for sewing up any tears. I don't know about tears, I had *tears* in my eyes and my nose kept running, while I did my cobbling-up. Unexpectedly, the red rubber gloves saved the day, I couldn't have coped other-wise. I only managed five minutes break for my lunch, no time to trek across the farm-yard to the privy. You couldn't leave a job half done.

That afternoon, young Katy went in the shop on my behalf – the shop assistant let out a little scream when she saw me hover-ing outside. 'You're not allowed in!' My fellow mums kept a wide berth. I staggered home, aching in every joint. I decided to use the boys' shower, because I wasn't sure I could make it upstairs...

The dreaded turkey sniffles struck me on the third day. I was committed to my work, so I took a man-size box of tissues with me and hoped for the best.

Then the snow began to fall. It drifted through the cracks and blew through the shed door whenever it was opened. We were all coughing now. On a couple of occasions, a visiting daughter came to my rescue, and helped poor old sick mum with her task. Sara was great at repairing any mishaps and Jo somehow managed to swap my giant half plucked monster with a smaller version left for a few moments on the table by one of the pluckers. He looked at it suspiciously on his return, but took it back to his seat with a sigh. At least our feet were warming up as promised, in the feather bed around our wellies. We didn't lose our needles in a hay-stack, rather a mound of feathers. The magnets weren't much help. When scissors, knives and even a wedding ring were seemingly lost forever, someone brought in a metal detector. They found the wedding ring, which was the most important.

I was on my third pair of Marigold gloves when the cry went up, 'We've done it!' We peeled off our gloves and went home. I was able to return to the school to pick up the children, smelling of lily of the valley perfume and wearing decent attire. But it took some days before I felt back to normal.

We were to be paid just before Christmas. I joined a long queue outside the farmhouse, one frosted white morning. We shuffled this time through thick snow, and we were only allowed into the pay office i.e. the kitchen, one at a time. No mince pies or mulled wine were on offer, not even a nice hot cup of coffee. I accepted my wages with numbed fingers and mumbled my appreciation. The list was checked, and I was asked to pay for my turkey, which could be collected a few days later. Despite the concession, I had only a few pounds left.

The twenty-five pound turkey hung in the hall of the chapel until Christmas Eve. Katy recalls looking at it fearfully, but Ginge immortalized it in a painting. One of us, I can't recall who, offered to hang it on their wall.

Those turkeys were beautiful specimens, and because I had seen the excellent conditions in which they were kept on the farm, and was aware they were humanely despatched when the time came, I felt I had achieved something in that shed... Some years later, I would actually become a champion turkey plucker – and that was quite an achievement, I can tell you!

There were more exotic feathers adorning a magnificent headdress. I was learning more about Boffy by the day. She was the younger, only surviving daughter of a Suffragette, and her sister had been a well-known dancer in her day. Boffy had inherited all her stage costumes, and these came out in turn for the

W.I. Christmas Party, whether fancy dress or no.

This year, Boffy wore a Minnie-Ha-Ha dress with a Hiawatha head band, with gorgeous coloured feathers. From this were suspended false black wool plaits. She had beaded moccasins on her feet. Who could possibly upstage that?

The staid committee ladies became flushed and sang and danced to the constant flow of tunes emanating from Millicent's flying fingers on the piano. I got over excited (on cups of tea) and was looked at reprovingly when I encouraged an elderly member to 'peel off!' during the Happy Ho Down. 'What *do* you mean?' she asked. We played silly games with pencil and paper, and dear Mrs B muttered away behind the hatch and kept the urn bubbling. She had a wicked sense of humour, and I enjoyed her little 'asides.' I also discovered that she had a lovely singing voice. We all stopped in our tracks once to listen as she serenaded the tea cups.

My friend Meg had received an invitation,

and she confided that she might change her mind, join the group sooner rather than later. There was another guest, the newly retired district nurse, and Girl Guide Commissioner, who had recently moved to the Mill estate. She and Meg were joint winners of the quiz game where the names of local places were scrambled – I suspected they might have played the game before, with the school children or the guides! Beatrice was another large, comfortable lady with a booming voice and she still had the health of the village at heart. She issued advice freely, which was not always appreciated. She had a hearing aid which emitted whistles at inopportune moments, like when she was in church.

It was no surprise when Beatrice was elected President at the next W.I. AGM. She and Boffy were a perfect team, even though they rubbed sparks off each other, being two strong minded single ladies. I was voted to serve on the committee as Press Secretary, much to my surprise, and I was pleased to learn that committee meetings were often held at Mrs B's house, where her nice husband waited for a lull in the conversation and then appeared with a loaded tea trolley! Oh, those feather-light sponges oozing with home-made strawberry jam... Alf cut such satisfying slices.

Four

You Can't teach an
Old Dog New Tricks
(I don't mean Billow, I mean me...)

It was Spring, and I was ready for a new challenge. I was approached this time by two long-time field workers who said they admired my fortitude in the turkey plucking shed! Would I like to join them in hop training? They assumed I was keen on gardening, well, the truth is I know how lucky I am that John and most of the children have a love of the great outdoors, and growing things. Wherever we have lived, John has made beautiful gardens, some large, some small, and I have appreciated them all.

I am inspired by rural pursuits in general. A group of us in the village met for the mid-week church service, taken by a lovely ancient retired vicar, full of fun, who confided that he used a black felt pen to 'fill in' the holes in his socks: 'My dear wife thinks it's a splendid idea!' We went afterwards to a grand house with a stream and a punt in the garden, and had a shared lunch there before embarking on various handicrafts. Every Christmas, John slyly brings out the snowman I made then from a cardboard tube and a long strip of bandage, and a rather wonky fairy fashioned from felt...

However, I had only a romantic view of 'hopping' days past. My good friend Liz actually made it sound idyllic. 'Each family had its own hut, and we little ones helped in our own way. We had sing-songs around a camp fire and sausages cooked on sticks held in the fire, for supper... We slept on mattresses filled with straw, and woke to the heady smell of hops and the prospect of another sunny, busy day...'

Liz's gran's had been one of the many families from the East End of London who spent their holidays in Kent picking the hops. She married a local lad and never went back.

So, I rashly said yes. My old clothes were clean and ready, my boots just needed a hose down. 'Hop garden' sounded just the job in fine weather.

I can't say to this day where the farm truck took us. I was picked up on the corner of Church hill after the children were safely deposited at school. They moaned a bit because they were not going along for the ride and 'the picnic' Mum would un-doubtedly enjoy later after a leisurely spot of *Firsting* i.e. training the tender shoots up the strings.

The truck had obviously been used for transporting pigs recently. Sacks were spread over the grubby straw for the workers to sit on as the truck lurched along narrow roads or jerked to a stop when confronted by a tractor. I was 'all shook up' and wondering if it was too far to walk home, when we bumped down a rutted lane for what seemed like a couple of miles, to a forest of hop poles. Our party of six descended from the tailboard on wobbly legs.

I longed for a cup of tea, but it wasn't yet nine a.m. A stocky man told us tersely that we were on piecework, which was bad news, only he didn't say that, of course, for beginners like me. 'You will be paid by the cant,' he added. What on earth was a cant? At least it was downhill all the way, I thought: my eyes glazed over at the endless marching poles. Where were the hops? Seeing my indecision, the foreman knew he had a rookie. He led me to my first pole. The four strings reminded me of a harp – would they twang if you plucked them?

'See these shoots? You train the strongest ones, two together up each string... The weaklings need to be pulled up, to give the others the best chance.' He then demonstrated the sequence to me, but his twirling of the shoots was so swift, I wasn't sure I could master the technique. 'Well, I'll leave you to it,' he said, and he rattled off in the truck. My companions were disappearing fast along their poles. I had no-one near enough to call on for advice.

How I wished John was with me. He was used to training runner beans, this would be a doddle for him. I took a deep breath and got down on my haunches – I already knew this was going to be backbreaking labour...

Well, I twiddled those darn shoots some one way, and some the other, whichever they seemed to prefer. The foreman hadn't told me they should be trained in a clockwise direction. Any good gardener would have known that, wouldn't they?

Around eleven, my legs were giving out. I collapsed on the ground. The sun beat down mercilessly on my head. I had retied my kerchief (we all wore them then, gypsy style; they were scraps of silk or cotton, brightly patterned) round the back of my neck to prevent sun stroke. I fumbled with my back pack, pulled out a banana and was just taking a bite, hoping it would give me the energy to carry on, when a booming voice startled me: 'Not time for a break yet!' I looked up to see a face glaring down at me. One of my fellow workers had spotted me and run over to reprimand me.

'Sorry...' I murmured faintly, struggling up and managing to crawl forward on my knees. Didn't they label workers like me 'Blacklegs'?

By the time I reached the bottom of the hill, I realized I was on my own. The others were enjoying their lunch, back at the top and were about to move on to pastures new. Literally, because the truck would pick them up and take them heaven knows where.

'Hurry up, Sheila!' came the call. I hadn't time to eat lunch, so I poured myself a cup of tea from my flask. Again, I looked up to see that I had broken an unwritten law. The foreman had been checking my progress.

'*You* ain't going nowhere,' he said brusquely. 'You've jiggered most of 'em up the wrong way!' He didn't say 'jiggered' either. 'You'll have to go back to the beginning and jigger 'em all the right way. Well, we're off. I'll pick you up at 3 o'clock, you should have finished by then.'

In fact, I never went back. I don't suppose they would have asked me to, anyway. No *Seconding*, *Thirding* and *Twiddling* for me. Having no head for heights, I couldn't have managed the last procedure which entailed climbing a ladder and using a wand with a prong on the end to do the final twiddling of the full-grown hops. I wasn't sacked, but you can still feel sorry for me, because the next morning both our young ones were poorly. They had gone down with chicken pox. They didn't have it mildly, as the older children had, in our orchard days, when, though in quarantine at home, they had enjoyed recovering mostly outdoors in the sunshine. Katy and Matthew had those horrible blisters mostly inside their mouths and throat – it was a virulent strain that year ... but I heard later it was a good year for hops.

Well, before you think what a wimp I am, before too long, I gained respect for my endeavours in an unexpected way.

I met a young red-haired mother with two little boys in the shop one day, and we got talking. She had only just arrived in the village and was feeling lonely. She invited me over to her house nearby for a cup of tea. She was a few years younger than me, but I've always had friends across the generations – age doesn't come into it.

We sat in the kitchen and I couldn't help commenting on the lovely smell of newly baked bread. Along the counter were stacked several loaves, mostly wholemeal, with crusty tops and a tray of rolls, twisted into attractive shapes.

'When we married, we decided to take on a bakery and make *real* bread,' Sue confided. 'My husband started work before dawn each day, to make and prove the dough. I went in later to make the cakes. We both worked until late afternoon, we didn't close the shop until the shelves were empty... We made a good team and we were doing really well. Then the babies came along, and I couldn't do all I did before to help him. He was so tired all the time, and we lost heart in the business. We had an offer for the bakery and the shop, and we decided we'd had enough. We still love baking–'

'I can see that,' I said, looking at the tempting loaves.

'But, we knew our marriage would suffer if we carried on. The children hardly saw their father, he was always working. So we came here because my husband is now a sales representative for a big firm.'

'Are you feeling better now?' I ventured.

'We're getting there... I was disappointed to find you have no playgroup here – it would be a good place for the children and me to make new friends. I've been looking into starting one up, but I can't do it on my own. I was a teacher before I married, but of secondary school children. *You* have plenty of experience with younger children, I'm relatively new to dealing with toddlers – would you like to be involved?'

I thought about it. Then I said, 'When we

lived on the smallholding and all the children were young, there were always other children round to play. My friend's two little girls almost lived at our place, she said she trusted me to look after them while she was working. The more the merrier, was my motto.'

'How about you and me working together? We could hire the village hall twice a week and do some fund-raising for equipment–'

'We'd need to canvass the village first, see if that's what they'd like,' I said. 'And wouldn't we need training?'

Sue nodded. 'I've already been into all that. You join the Preschool Playgroup Association and do a course. You have to have a Police check, and a health check, too. You need a certificate in first aid. It'll take a few months to set up, but we'd have to do it properly. When it's up and going you need a team of volunteers to help – and really, we could do with someone like a nursery nurse or an ex-teacher in the team.'

'I'll ask around, as I know more people

than you, from the school run,' I offered.

'I don't think there will be much possibility of being paid ourselves, does that worry you, Sheila?'

'Some jobs you do for love,' I said.

I went home, walking on air, with a warm loaf of bread in my bag. Training toddlers was more my style than training hops, wasn't it?

Five

Boys and Girls Come Out to Play

We began with notes through letterboxes, coffee mornings and mum's meetings, and it seemed to us that there was a real need among the local children to get together to play, learn and have fun.

Sue had done her homework: as prospective supervisors we had to be thoroughly vetted by the local authority; the village hall had to pass a stringent fire hazard test and we embarked on fund raising for equipment. We also joined the Pre-School Playgroups Association.

There was now a third member of our team, Marcia, who was taking a sabbatical from teaching science in a comprehensive school. I was to add to their expertise my experience of bringing up and amusing a large family, and I suspect, to add the motherly touch – you know, taking children to the loo, or coping with Lolly, who's been screaming blue murder since her mum went.

We had great fun, once a week, planning our two sessions. Children thrive on a mix of familiarity, stimulation, firmness and importantly, in my view, imagination. We adapted, modified and approved our ideas as we went along. It was physically hard work as some of the play equipment was heavy and had to be stored in what was usually an inconvenient place. Try lifting from a height a plastic pit filled to the brim with soft, golden sand – and buried treasure!

Everything had to be put away neatly at the end of each session, too. We hopefully issued a rota of helpful mums at the start of each term, but it was surprising how it always seemed to be the faithful few who kept turning up.

'Most mums,' Sue said, 'open the hall door, shove their children inside and beat a hasty retreat!' They claimed that if they lingered longer, the children just clung tighter. They had a point! However, we didn't really mind. Some of them obviously needed the break.

I will now give you the lowdown on a typical playgroup day! Around this time I was writing a series of articles on family life, the highs and lows, for *My Weekly* magazine. I've just found a cache of these mags. They read like a diary, in the present tense. I am happy to say that it really was as I recall it now, so I'll continue in the same vein...

8.45 a.m. Family has departed, washing-up is done, beds pulled together, dust on the mantelpiece ignored, ditto overflowing wash basket, and I have seen Katy and Maff into school. I have a bagful of playgroup para-phernalia, along with the register and hall key.

At 8.55 a.m. I collect four pints of milk from the hall step and open up. Then Marcia arrives, sensibly attired in her uniform of ancient jeans and baggy jumper which, she proudly informs me is the only thing she has ever knitted – fifteen years ago, in her teens! She really doesn't look much older than that now, being small and slight, I think. We work very well together. We arrange the tables and chairs around the hall and unroll a large gymnastic mat.

Into the tiny corner of the storeroom we venture at 9.10 a.m. We select the table activities of the day. Whilst Marcia puts out the building bricks, jigsaws, blunt scissors, crayons, paper, old wallpaper pattern books, I arrange the book corner, with little chairs circled invitingly around. Then we mix up plain flour, cooking oil, colouring, salt and water into a lovely pliable lump of play dough.

The first children arrive along with Sue and her own two little ones, at 9.20 a.m. She assembles the slide and small chute, tumbles bricks out on to the mat, spreads a large sheet of plastic to hopefully catch the drips from the painting easels, goes into the kitchen to put on the kettle, sets out the coffee cups and mixes more paint.

We know it's 9.30 a.m. when the door is flung wide, and in they all troop! Sue copes with the register and money. Marcia greets any newcomers and I unbutton coats, stuff gloves into pockets, slip plastic aprons over often-protesting heads and peg up painting paper. One or two mums linger, nostrils twitching at the aroma of coffee.

In the winter, we're in the hall from 9.30 until 10 a.m. but if it's fine, we go outside into the small garden, with the sandpit.

The older, bolder children move from table to table. Ruth is the exception. She concentrates on the jigsaws, sometimes assembling them upside-down, but doesn't socialise with the other children. Toby gets in a sly dig with a pencil at Ben. Ellen gets her long hair tugged. Rosy, blowing into a mixture of paint and washing-up liquid in a mug through a straw to make bubbles, sucks by mistake and splutters!

The more boisterous children queue impatiently for the chute. This, and the mini-trampoline need constant supervision.

When tears and tantrums develop, I suggest music. Marcia puts her hands over her ears and wears a pained expression. I fetch out the elderly record player, our few records and the musical instruments – some home made.

We twang an elastic band across an empty tissue box, rub sandpaper blocks together, rattle lentils in a plastic bottle, play a comb-and-paper and bang a sweet-tin drum. After 10 minutes of cacophony and dervish-twirling I confiscate the instruments of torture and decide to remove my lot farther down the hall for some play-acting.

Sometimes we go the moon, 'Pull on your boots, zip up your spacesuits, fasten your seat-belts – three, two, one, blast off!' But today we fancy a visit to the old witch of the woods.

'Tie up your horses,' I say, when we've galloped over to the clearing where the old witch is stirring her cauldron and making spells. We stir vigorously, too and chant, *Iddy, Oddy, Idey, Og*, let's all become a hopping frog!' We hop about and get into trouble for knocking against Toby's castle of bricks and demolishing it.

'Time to clear up!' Marcia calls. We all stack the table-toys, admire the paintings and lay them out to dry. We always feel sorry when impatient mums can't wait to take home the latest 'Picasso'.

By 10.45 the tables are formed into an L shape. The children drink their milk and munch their biscuits. We sing 'Happy Birthday' to Giles, who is four.

Now for Marcia's speciality. On an easel she has pinned a picture of an old, sad-looking woman, wrapped up in a shawl and wearing a huge apron with a pinned-on pocket. 'What do you think we are going to sing?' she asks brightly.

'There was an Old Woman who swallowed a Fly!' someone shouts and they trot up in turn to deposit the various unlikely objects they sing about into the bulging pocket. Until – 'She's swallowed a horse!' and Toby shouts in relief, 'She's dead, of course!'

because he can't wait for Big Toy Time. Another song follows, this time 'Five Little Spotted Frogs, Sat on a Spotted Log.' It's a great favourite, and we illustrate that too, with a super picture painted by Ginge, as part of her teacher training course.

11 a.m. now, time for the Special Activity! If a big occasion looms up like Mother's Day, we get out the glue and make sticky cards with coloured paper or tissue, sticking on feathers or pasta. Sometimes, we make something to illustrate a song, perhaps cut out 'Nelly the Elephant', poke our fingers through the hole in the face, wiggle them for her trunk and then dance and sing around the hall. Or I am asked: 'Please can we have one of your tapes, Sheila?' Several of my short stories for small children are on cassettes produced for playgroups. An added bonus is, I receive free tapes for our own group. Their favourite (and mine!) is *Toffee Cakes on Tuesday*, to which the presenters have added a catchy song. (I sometimes wonder if any of my earlier bedtime stories

for the Hull Telephone Company, for which I received 7s. 6d each, were ever recorded...)

However, today we have a Great Activity planned and several mums have been enlisted to help. We're going to record our footprints!

One mum supervises the taking off of socks and shoes while another mum lines up the children. Little ones first, they can't wait... In a tray Sue has poured some bright blue paint, Marcia and I unroll a long, long piece of lining paper, Toby's mum is poised with a marking pen, and finally a mum crouches over a bowl of soapy water, with towels nearby.

Tina steps in first. A tiny foot-print is recorded. Minnie's next, red eyed and runny-nosed because she is not No. 1. The line is fairly well-behaved, but there's some shoving from the rear. George dives for the tray of paint, slips up and rolls in it. He's smothered in blue from head to foot. George's mum gathers him up and rushes him to the kitchen sink. The bubbles soon turn blue, and suddenly the fun's gone out of the whole affair. Marcia goes to help. The rest of us send the remaining children smartly through the process, clear up and sigh with relief.

It's now 11.25 a.m. and the hall's cleared. From the grubby recesses beneath the stage, we bring out the big toys. Most children get the car, bike or rocker of their choice, and the milk-float, as usual is the most popular.

'Three turns round the hall,' we say firmly to Lolly, 'Then give it to Toby.'

Two of us supervise, while the other clears up the kitchen and begins tidying away. The noise level is horrific – but they all look so happy!

Story time follows at 11.45. It's Sue's turn today. Like little angels they sit quietly in a circle, listening. The first mums tiptoe into the hall, and listen, too. The story is an old favourite, all about a giant jam sandwich which captures a plague of wasps. I start to feel hunger pangs. We then button up coats and buttonhole mums.

'Don't forget we're going swimming at the Sports centre, next Tuesday. We need helpers for the walk to see the lambs the following Tuesday. Yes, I know we have to negotiate that dangerous stretch before we turn up the lane, but we've got a length of rope. What for? Oh, well, you'll see, but it works I assure you! Bye, bye.'

Then it's just us three and it's noon. We sweep up the hall. 'Look at all those cigarette ends,' Marcia says indignantly. 'That's not us,' and 'Ugh! More chewing gum! I had to take some out of Rosy's mouth. She told me she found it stuck to the radiator. The Youth Club make more mess than our little ones do!' 'Did you tell Rosy's mum?' 'Er. No, do you think I should have?' We forget it.

I go home to my bread and cheese. I can't wait for liver and onions. But as I unwind, I think: I had a great day – despite George's slip into the blue!

Well, Marcia and I continued to enjoy the

challenges and catastrophes for over four years, after Sue and her family moved away a year after we set up the playgroup. We had great support from a regular team of mothers, including one mum, with a small daughter who was 'doing it all again,' she told us with a smile, as her elder daughter was sixteen and her son a teenager when little Nicola was born. This was June, who has been my dear friend since those days, as you will see from the dedication to this book, and later chapters... Time for a new team.

Out of the blue, I was offered a new challenge – you'll hear about that later!

Six

Wedding bells

There were eleven of us in the minibus, just like old times. Not JP, as we were joining him in Suffolk, for he and Di were to be married tomorrow, but we had collected his best man, Graham, en route. We travelled on the Friday evening, after work and school. I had to call the boys in from the football field when John said it was time to go. They had their own bags ready packed. I should have checked that Roger had included his new black shoes to go with his best clothes for the wedding. Half way through the journey he realized that the shoes were still in their box at home, and that he was wearing disreputable old trainers. 'I didn't say anything then, as it was too far to go back,' he confessed on our arrival. We would need to go out early next morning to buy him another pair. We were miles from the nearest town, so had to pin our hopes on the local Co-op.

Some of us were staying with Jonathan in the cottage which went with his job on the dairy farm, but the girls, including Katy, who were to be bridesmaids, together with Di's younger sisters, were staying nearby with the same dear aunt with whom we lived during the war. We had Billow with us. He was our only pet at the moment, as Tiger, our ginger cat had 'faded away' quietly last summer at fifteen years old.

JP and Di had been very busy in their limited off-duty hours – Di was a nursery nurse – they had decorated their Victorian cottage and begun to tackle the wilderness of garden. On the kitchen wall Jonathan had painted his own version of the popular newspaper cartoon, *Love Is...* They were our own ideal young couple, we thought fondly, when we saw this tribute to his bride. Di had filled the shelves with pottery, she was already amassing a collection of china cockerels with bright plumage, also cooking pots – even then, she was a splendid cook.

They had big plans for the garden, we just knew that some time soon, a menagerie would appear just as it had with us, in our orchard days!

Three very important family members would be missing from this happy celebration. John's mother had sadly passed away a year or so back. It was a great loss to us all. I always say I had the perfect mother-in-law. My own father was very frail at almost ninety, and now bedridden following a stroke, and my mum could not leave him. JP and Di had decided that their wedding should be on Oz's (that's what I called my dad) birthday in March.

None of us guessed how cold it would be on the east coast, with bitter winds blowing. Di's mum had to rustle up enough jumpers for the girls to wear under their pretty bridesmaids' frocks. Not quite the Spring wedding we had visualised.

The boys had spent the night in their sleeping bags in the living room. They went out with JP at dawn to watch him milk the cows and to help with the feeding. Matthew and Billow reluctantly stayed indoors with us. The farm chores still had to be done, but JP was being allowed the rest of the day off! John cooked bacon and eggs all round. The fire was lit, but it was a dark, dank morning.

After breakfast, John, Matthew and I took a reluctant Roger shopping. The only acceptable (in Roger's eyes) footwear available was a pair of white trainers. Hardly the shoes to wear to a wedding, but preferable to the now muddy ones he had on. We were running short on time, and parted with a fiver for this bargain.

Chris and Michael were actually spruced up by the time we returned to the cottage. Graham had taken them in hand, as Jonathan was nowhere to be seen. He'd been called back to the farm to help deal with an emergency, they told us. We learned later it was a calving.

There was less than an hour to go before the wedding. John and I tried to keep calm, but there wasn't anything we could do, except get changed into our finery. Graham was hovering in the background. Poor chap, I thought; all this family stuff must be a shock to the system.

With half an hour to go, we had to leave for the church. We knew that the girls had been fetched earlier from my aunt's and taken to the bride's home. They would be well looked after by Di's lovely mum, Daphne. Graham waited for the bridegroom and promised us they'd arrive at the church before the bride... Fortunately, as we settled in the minibus, Jonathan appeared. From the look of him he would need a good bath. Had he got time for that? We waved at him, laughing in relief. 'Good luck – see you in church!' we called, crossing fingers.

All the guests had arrived, despite the weather. We hurried into the little country church tucked away 'in the middle of nowhere', and John and I and Maff were shown to our pew at the front. The organ was playing and the bride would shortly arrive, but there was no sign yet of the bridegroom and the best man... I got down on my knees and said a fervent little prayer.

'They're here!' the whisper went round. There was a palpable sigh of general relief. John squeezed my hand, he guessed I had tears in my eyes.

Then I almost had a fit of the giggles, because as our son stood waiting with his back to us, I saw that his wet hair was dripping on his collar. He hadn't had time to dry it.

Heads turned, the organ pealed, and Diane, in a beautiful white gown made by her mother, with auburn ringlets tucked under her veil, came slowly down the aisle on her father's arm, followed by her six bridesmaids in blue. Di was only nineteen, Jonathan was twenty-two, and their faces glowed with happiness. Somehow, we all felt warmer, despite the weather.

Later, after the photographer had done his bit, we all repaired to the village hall and to a veritable feast, crowned by a wonderful wedding cake. I can't tell you what we ate, because the rest of the afternoon seems like a dream. It all went smoothly, despite the early morning setbacks.

We returned home to Kent that evening. The bridegroom, after Sunday morning milking, and his bride left to spend their honeymoon in Surrey staying with my parents. Apparently, they took their cases upstairs and changed into their wedding clothes. Mum and Dad were thrilled and touched to see them just as they had looked, the day before, and dear Di presented my mother with her wedding bouquet.

At the time of writing this, my mother is 101 years old! JP and Di are still very close to her, in fact JP visits her every day after work and does her shopping. (She moved back to her native Suffolk after my father died.) They have now been married thirty years, it hardly seems possible! We have had eight family weddings to date, but Katy is the last one of our children about to tie the knot! John and I have made wedding cakes for most of these, but fortunately, as we have got out of the way of cooking for large numbers in recent years, she has decreed a chocolate cake!

A year and a half later, in September, there was another celebration – our Silver Wedding Anniversary! We made the traditional cake and were so excited we found ourselves telling everyone, 'Open House!' Boffy heard about the party on the grapevine – courtesy of Katy and Matthew. They ran ahead of me as we wended our way home from school each day to hear all the village news before I did. Recently, she'd held out a glass Kilner jar containing some unidentifiable black objects floating in what looked like brine. 'Found this jar lurking in the cupboard under the sink,' she said, 'I thought it was time it was used up. I might have the contents for my supper...'

'But, Boffy – what are they?' *Botulism*, I thought.

'Could be tomatoes, could be plums – luck of the draw, m'dear. I just need you to unscrew the top of the jar for me. I asked the man working over the road, but he wouldn't do it.

'Go on, Mum!' chorused my offspring.

Naturally I didn't try very hard, and suggested she dispose of it. A few days later, Boffy told me triumphantly, 'I got it open!'

'You didn't...' I asked apprehensively.

'I had them, whatever they were, on toast. Very nice!' Boffy said. (I couldn't resist using this little story, much later in my book *The Family at Number Five!)*

Now, I confirmed that she would be very welcome to pop in like other village friends 'for a piece of cake, and a Toast.' The other new friends took us at our word, and did just that; we were pleased to see them, but the chapel was overflowing with our extended family, including uncles, aunts, cousins, some with small children, and our

85

siblings with five nephews, and our niece, Penny, newly married herself. There were old school friends with us, too.

We had a running buffet all day. The boys operated the soft drinks soda stream, wisely hiding Boffy's homemade ginger beer, which Roger had sampled and then exclaimed, *'Poison!'* John sliced a whole large turkey and home-cooked ham. I'd invested in two giant glass bowls for our favourite raspberry trifle. Roger had presented us with a huge silver-coloured teapot, which needed a packet of tea every time we brewed it. We had to buy a display cabinet for all the silver trays, magnificent tea set and other items we were given. Quite a contrast with the 22 tablecloths we'd received as wedding gifts, but then times were still austere, ten years after the war.

Mum and Dad were, of course, unable to come, and we planned to visit them shortly and have a mini-celebration with them then. I'm so glad we did, because we lost our wonderful Oz three months later, on Christmas Day.

However, on our anniversary there were several elderly relatives who could not recall meeting each other before. I remember John's Uncle Tom joining the long queue for the toilet facilities and his cheerful cry of 'Make Way For The Walking Wounded!' And a cousin telling us, 'I have just had a very interesting conversation with your marvellous old aunt – the one in the sun hat – d'you know I couldn't for the life of me remember her name...' We saw the lady referred to, holding court in the garden. It was our friend Boffy, dressed up for the occasion in magenta satin with a lace jabot. (I was not quite so grand, but very pleased with the pretty pink frock presented to me by Jo.) Boffy had been among the first arrivals in the morning, and this was late afternoon.

Too soon after our arrival at the chapel, a new estate had sprung up in the wilderness around us, although fortunately for the boys, the playing field remained sacrosanct. Although we missed the daisies and dandelions and the long grass beyond our plot, there was a car park adjacent to the side of our garden, beyond the stout fence we had erected. Chris was now living away from home on his second farm placing before going to agricultural college, and Michael was doing well at his engineering apprenticeship in the nearby town. Both boys had their first small cars, so the car park was good news for them! On this day, visitors from afar were also glad to have somewhere to park off the road. (There's usually a silver lining to a drawback, isn't there?)

It was such a happy day and the chapel was the perfect place for a big party. The last pot of tea was made and dispensed among the remaining guests after the cake had been cut. The crowd thinned out, and the washing up and filling black sacks with paper plates and crumpled paper napkins began. It was getting towards dusk, when we decided the garden would have to wait until the morning. We were all ready to fall into bed after a day which had been busy since dawn. Glancing out of the window, I exclaimed: 'Oh, no!'

'What's up?' John asked, yawning. 'You're not going out there again to tidy up. Enough's enough.' He was already in his dressing gown and slippers. The family had all retired to their rooms.

'No, it isn't,' I said faintly, pointing at a shrouded object in the gloom. 'Boffy is asleep in the deckchair – didn't anyone notice?'

'There's going to be a moon,' he said hopefully. 'We put a rug round her knees earlier when it got nippy. Don't you think–'

'No!' I said. I saw he was grinning. He didn't mean it.

'I'll get dressed again, and take her home. You win,' John said.

He guided her gently up the road, opened her door, switched on the lights. 'Goodnight, Boffy. Off to your bed now, eh?'

'It was a lovely party, thank you. You made my day,' she said.

Dear Boffy, you made our day, too, bless you.

Seven

No Cup of Tea for Rosy Lee?

A big fete was planned to take place on the village green one August to raise money for the village hall refurbishment and the coming 800th celebration year of our parish church. Representatives of the many village organisations were roped in on the committee. Marcia and I represented the playgroup and John and Bill were involved too. We were a large committee, all eager to contribute ideas, so it was fortunate that Ian, the ever tactful but firm chairman was in charge.

A fancy dress parade for the children, suggested Meg. Here, Boffy suggested brightly, 'Couldn't we all be in costume?' It was hastily agreed that this should be optional.

The local Music-makers quartet was mooted by Millicent. She was the only female member, and was firmly established as their leader. The village policeman liked the idea of a motor cycle line-up. (A chance for him to check local lads' machines?) Ian's friend Ben volunteered to run a hot dog stall. That brought the suggestion of a dog show. John and Bill offered to take turns in a Dancing Bear costume with a hurdy gurdy. They didn't take into consideration that it might be a hot day and a fur suit could be claustrophobic. Mrs B was, as always, put in charge of the tea tent and cakes. Suddenly, the attention turned to me. 'What about you, Sheila?' was the challenge. A pause, then came inspiration (or was it?) 'I told fortunes once – oh, years ago–' I said. The committee were enthusiastic. I was promised a small tent, a goldfish bowl (empty) as a crystal sphere, and the costume and the spiel were up to me. It was decided, just like that...

Katy was really excited when she heard

about it. 'Oh, Mum, I'll do your makeup and help you dress up – me and Maff will make you a chart, so you can look up all the signs, Gemini and that,' (This was her birth sign) 'They are all in my comic, this week!' She was right, there was a double-page spread. I also recalled the long ago summer when my cousin and I found a well-thumbed paper-back on palmistry and tea-cup reading, 'for afternoon tea parties', which we pored over for hours, and then practiced by 'reading' the palms of willing, or unwilling, relatives and school friends. We both had a talent for telling stories, so no-one believed us.

Everyone will know it's me, I thought, and I'll only say nice things. It must be 'just for fun.' (Here I have to admit that a gypsy friend once told me I would be famous when I was old, so I've always had hopes, but it ain't happened yet! Well, getting older has, but not world-wide acclaim.)

John and Bill put up the flags around the green. They helped erect the tents. John had made a hurdy gurdy box with a handle to turn, and concealed a cassette player inside. The tape played real hurdy gurdy music. The bear costume was very realistic, and yes, stifling to wear. They were both over six feet in height, so with the bear head on top looked even taller. They planned to take half hour stints inside it. By eleven o'clock in the morning of the Big Day the smell of frying onions from the hot dog stall, and drifts of smoke pervaded the village, and sent folk hurrying for the midday opening.

The fete was opened by our very own Beauty Queen, Ian and Judy's gorgeous daughter. There was a rival attraction in the Strong Man, who had once been in Meg's class. He'd developed muscles since then and a crowd of admiring girls soon gathered round him. Meg observed drily in my ear: 'I was stronger than him in those days!'

In the cool, dark interior of my tent, I tried to memorize my astrology. I could hear the music and the laughter and was aware of folk brushing past my tent, and the aroma of onions and hot dogs grew stronger as a breeze wafted these in my direction. For the first half-an-hour I had no customers at all. I considered retrieving the sign, *Rosy Lee and her Crystal Ball. Consultations 50p*, and amending it to 30p a session.

I hope I looked the part, with my long hair plaited, gold hoop earrings (curtain rings – I don't have pierced ears) a shawl, an embroidered blouse and one of my Indian cotton skirts. Marcia had actually done my makeup as she had a box of greasepaints. I hoped I was unrecognisable, like my husband sweating away in his hired fur costume. He and Bill already had a satisfactory jingling in their collecting box for the day's good cause. The Quartet played valiantly, seated in a circle rather too near the dog show, so had to compete with a chorus of barks. The Bobby tut-tutted over the motor cycles and offered advice. Our neighbour had turned up in fancy dress, rather puzzling, for he was wearing swimming trunks and wellington boots, or maybe he was just catering for both sunshine and showers...

I was longing for a cup of tea, when the tent flap parted and in came my first customer. I had seen her picture in the paper recently. I knew she had a title, that she had a holiday mansion on the outskirts of the village, but that was all.

She smiled at me. 'Would you like to read my palm?' She held out a beautifully manicured hand, with a diamond ring sparkling above her wedding band. My own hands contrasted with hers. The old palmistry book had the low-down on hand shapes. Mine were not artistic (although I fondly imagined I was) – I was disappointed to discover that I had 'mechanic's hands'. My family would dispute that! The hand I now gazed upon would have fitted the 'lady' category.

Her voice was soft and sweet, with a captivating accent. Her blonde hair gleamed and her face was reflected in my crystal ball.

'You do not come from round here...' I began. I knew that much from the article in the paper.

'Ah, you know who I am?' she queried.

'I believe so...' The words spilled out from my sub-conscious. 'You were a dancer?' (I certainly had not read that information.) 'Ballet,' I continued.

'Yes, but that was a long time ago,' she said. She sounded sad. 'In my own country.'

She nodded in agreement at every statement I made. 'This is true.'

It was an uncanny experience for me, too. She smiled and said 'Goodbye and thank you.' I had earned my first fifty pence.

I was still bemused when I became aware that there was a long queue outside my tent. They must have been attracted by my first client, certainly not by me! I snapped into action and enjoyed the next couple of hours or so. Giggling girls and red-faced boys, stout matrons and twinkly eyed grandfathers, including my neighbour, still in his peculiar get up. The music had ceased: I emerged at last from my tent and discovered that the stall holders were packing up, the crowds going home to tea. 'Sorry,' Ben said, 'One of the dogs ate the last sausage...' as he dismantled the hot dog stand and scattered a broken bap to the ducks on the pond. The tea urn was likewise empty. 'My dear,' Mrs B said, concerned, 'Didn't anyone bring you a cup of tea?' I shook my head wearily. I looked around for the Russian bear, but he and Bill were counting their takings. Our children had gone home with their older siblings, to feed Billow and to have their own tea. Billow had not been dog show material and had wisely stayed in the chapel.

My friend claimed the crystal ball, and I rolled up the astrology map. You won't be surprised to know I have it still. I handed over my glass jar with the slit in the cover. It was crammed full of silver pieces.

That was the beginning and end of my brief career as Rosy Lee. You see, I couldn't help wondering why it was I had been so accurate in my predictions ... something not to meddle with, as my dear old Dad would say. It made me think of a story he'd told me once, and what happened when we delved deeper...

Dad's mother was the grandma-I-never-knew. I felt I did, because Dad told us so many stories of his unconventional childhood, first on the Isle of Sheppey (his father was in the Navy) and later when his mother ran a theatrical boarding house in Brixton. Oh, those wonderful music hall characters of the late Victorian and Edwardian era! My grandma sighed over moonlight flits by boarders who couldn't pay the rent: some left goods in lieu of this, like a violin, an oil painting, a trunk full of costumes, but she didn't bank on a pair of toddlers left in her care, whom she cared for over many years, until they were grown up. Jane, my dad called his mother fondly. So I felt I knew her, and she is very much part of my first published novel, *Tilly's Family* (or *The Family under the Sea Wall*.) I have her household remedies books and recipes from the turn of the last century until the 1930's and they are invaluable when I am writing of that era.

Jane was considered to be 'fey.' She had a

Spanish grandmother (like Jane, and Dad, I have inherited her dark eyes and so have five of our children and many of the grand-children) and the family home had been in Cornwall. Dad had visited there as a boy and remembered it well. When we were in the west country ourselves, he asked us to find out if the farmhouse was still there. He told me that Jane had experienced a vivid dream once about 'hidden treasure' buried in the garden there, in the 18th century, 'near an oak tree, with a rope swing.' He wondered if this had ever been verified...

Well, we found the farm, and we also discovered that the old churchyard was full of Jane's ancestors, including one with the intriguing Christian name of Arminal! A lovely elderly couple, now retired from farming, told us they had lived there since their marriage. Over cups of tea and hot buttered scones, I mentioned the mystery.

They took us out into the garden. There was the ancient oak, and the now frayed ropes of a long-gone swing. 'Our son was digging here, when his spade struck something hard,' the old farmer told us. 'It was an enormous stone slab and he couldn't shift it. The grass has grown over it since.' He poked about with his stick. 'We heard the rumours, but thought it was best not to try to find out.'

We agreed, but it was uncanny to think we had found the place in Jane's dream. Actually, John probably hit on the truth when he said later to me, 'I think it was actually an ancient cess pit. In that case, who would want to shift that great stone?'

I didn't say, of course, but I believe Jane would have wanted to gaze into the depths, and yes, in a holding-my-breath sort of way, so would I.

Eight

'Gorillas', Grapes and a Ticket to Rye

Time for you to meet June! We were in a lush part of the Weald of Kent, overflowing with cherry and apple orchards, hops, and yes, strawberry fields. We were also not far from the coast and quaint little towns like Rye, with its harbour and fascinating shops. This was H.E. Bates country, not too far from where the Larkins had their genesis. H.E. is still one of my favourite authors.

June's youngest, Nicola, called Nik, had just started school, so June and I teamed up for a holiday (or so we thought) in the sun, picking (and eating) strawberries just a lorry ride away from home. We had a lot in common: her elder daughter was an artist, like Sara and Virginia. ('What about us?' the rest

101

of the family might well remind me. They are certainly creative too, as you may have gathered from their proud mum! It's in the genes, as they say.) June's Debbie had already drawn the captivating little bear who featured in the *Forever Friends* cards and spin-off stationery. June loved books, like me – she had worked as a librarian before she married.

Neither of us were natural field workers, but gave our utmost to the cause for little reward. That sounds sanctimonious – sorry! But we did do our best, honestly. June is now an accomplished gardener, while I like looking up from the keyboard and gazing out at the flowers with pleasure, from time to time.

We had what appeared to be an inter-changeable wardrobe of ancient trousers, drab anoraks and wellington boots. As we both wore glasses, had fair hair and burned in the sun, we even looked alike. We were not the sort of strawberry pickers who stripped down to bra and shorts, but then none of the team were remotely like that either. There were ancient pickers, surprisingly nimble, and skinny girls who loped along the rows and filled their punnets with the biggest and best fruits. There were young mums who grumbled a lot and took cigarette breaks under the hedge when the farmer wasn't looking. June and I suspected that a couple of these women 'lifted' a tray or two from the piled up boxes at the end of our rows, while we were toiling at the far end, but we couldn't prove it. The mums also had small children in tow, some still in nappies, not always well behaved, but then they were not allowed to play hide and seek among the rows and were bored. *'Shut up!'* was the clarion call.

The rows of strawberries stretched out of sight and by midday we were down on our knees, crawling in the straw. After the first day, I took a cushion. My knees were flattened and raw. Once or twice we fell among the strawberries and felt like lying there until we were missed a week or so later. It was cooler among the green foliage, though the straw pricked our arms and legs, and we squashed a few berries to the horror of the man sent to see what we were up to. He issued a warning. I actually retaliated with, 'We can't be expected to work in these conditions. The toilet is disgusting.' The shed which seemed to be miles from the field housed a bucket with a plank over it. The man scowled. 'You're not supposed to go there, unless you *have* to,' he said tersely. We were speechless.

We knew the technique, brushing a hand among the leaves, feeling for clusters of fruit; only picking the reddest and mixing small berries with large. Any we 'plugged' – well we ate the evidence. The problem was, this was a new variety of strawberries, delicious but huge and hard with stalks which we had to wrestle with, between finger and thumb, before they snapped. We were told by one of the overseers that these were Gorillas. Well, that's what it sounded like, began with a G anyway. But Gorillas they certainly were, and our fingers were really sore by the end of the afternoon. They were stained too, and I had to buy a pair of white gloves to wear to a social occasion at John's head office. Have you ever tried eating 'nibbles' with gloves on?

Things did improve, and so did the weather. We actually made cotton squares into halter-neck sun tops and wore floppy hats like Boffy. We were still glad of something to kneel on, for the straw was harder and more brittle by the day. We felt proud that our strawberries were destined to be eaten at Wimbledon, and we topped each punnet with the biggest and juiciest of all, with perfect green 'caps.' When Sara wrote to tell us that she had spent her birthday queuing for hours with fellow students from the art college to watch the tennis, and that they had a celebration lunch of strawberries and cream, I wondered if they had been 'our' gorillas... I should have hidden a little note in the punnets, rather as women did who knitted socks for soldiers: 'Picked by

Mum x'

We were accepted by the gang, and told that, unofficially, we were allowed to fill our empty lunch boxes with small strawberries to take home for our family. 'But you must only do this in your lunch break, when you aren't paid to pick.' I was very popular at supper time at home. Good old Mum! I did spend much of my earnings on cream from the farm, though. The strange thing is, I had been allergic to strawberries as a child, they brought me out in hives, but eating them fresh like that I was fine. I liked them best without sugar and cream.

I recovered from my initial dismay at the conditions I was working under, though neither June nor I would join the others 'hopping behind the hedge.' We just tried not to think about calls of nature. It was so different from the *Knee Deep in Plums* days when I'd so enjoyed picking strawberries in a small field up the lane, with Katy in her pram under a canopy, and five-year old Roger filling the trays with punnets for me.

I was among friends there and I could pop home when necessary. Here, though, I was doing a real job, I was fitter and tanned at the end of it, and my hair was bleached blonde at the tips. We were also invited to pick the plants clean at the end of the season, for free! Then I was stirring strawberry jam in the pot. A whole army of jars marched along the kitchen shelf, but I knew the family would soon thin out the ranks.

Later in the year June and I joined the grape pickers. This was a model vineyard, with proper loos and respect for the workers. Lunch breaks were leisurely affairs, because free bottles of wine were dispensed by the owner. As non-imbibers, it amused us to see the soporific effect this had on some of our fellow pickers. We were paid by the hour, so although we worked steadily, there was no sense of urgency.

We moved along the vines, secateurs in hand, and the laden sprays of grapes nestled in the buckets at our feet. Every now and again, a nice man, bent almost double under the weight of a huge bin strapped to his back, paused by each picker to request: 'Would you be kind enough to empty your bucket into the bin? Thank you very much.'

We couldn't eat the grapes because they had been treated with what looked like a fine white powder. We wore gloves so that we didn't come into contact with this. We were shown the various processes, where the grapes were washed and then crushed. June and I wished we could tread them as they used to do in France!

One day a TV camera crew arrived to film us. A single mum who worked with us, was terrified she would be spotted by 'the powers that be'. She lurked in the loos (clean, sparkling and sweet smelling) until the crew had gone. We felt for the poor girl, trying to hush her children.

This really was a break for us, and we thoroughly enjoyed the grape picking. At half-term Katy, Maff and little Nik came along with us, and they had a great time, too. My two played with the small girl on a lovely lush spread of grass under shady trees. Children were welcome here. The vineyard folk were great. Matthew recalls that the youngsters were invited to pick juicy Spartan apples from the trees in the meadow, and take some home, too. Scrumping permitted – wonderful!

Before they went back to school, I had time at home with the children. Roger usually came in for lunch, but today he would be invited into the kitchen of kind Mrs Greengrass, the farmer's wife. She made chocolate cake especially for his elevenses. He had stepped into brother Chris's shoes, well, boots, on a local farm with the intention to follow him in due course to agricultural college.

Katy, Maff and I took the bus along the winding lanes, past oast houses and white boarded cottages, through all the little villages in a roundabout route to Rye. It was a special excursion ticket, we picked up passengers at every stop, and a lovely day out. We came at last to the harbour, where Rye's fleet of fishing boats was moored, bobbing in the sun-dappled water by the Salts, grassland which in times gone by was purposely flooded with sea water, Following evaporation, salt deposits were collected and used in preserving the catches of fish. Time to disembark! We took the short cut into town, mingling with the crowd from the bus, then dispersed in various directions.

Rye is so soaked in history with tales of smugglers, like the Hawkurst Gang who frequented the *Mermaid Inn*, with loaded pistols at the ready beside their tankards of ale. We toiled up and down the steep cobbled street, peeping in the leaded windows of the Inn and looking across to *The House Opposite*, aptly named, as was *The House With a Seat*, (in the porch), which was next door to *The House Without a Seat*. The children loved all those names. It was like stepping back into Medieval times, we always had an eerie feeling, in Mermaid Street.

We couldn't see all the sights on one visit,

but we admired the Landgate, the remaining entrance to the town. Our guide book told us that this was built in the 14thC and restored and strengthened after the French sacked and burned all the wooden structures in the town in 1377. Rye, we were aware, was one of the Cinque Ports and played a vital role in the defence of the coast from attack by the French. We saw the old Grammar School, now a private dwelling, 'It couldn't have had many pupils,' observed Maff. From the outside, it appeared that the rooms inside were tiny.

They were keen to spend their pocket money, so we visited the Rye Pottery. The china was beautiful, but all we could afford was a blue and white egg-cup apiece! Another fascinating shop was packed with ephemera. Bags of marbles, amazing working models and old-fashioned toys which we took time to enjoy and select. I bought a clockwork mechanism for a musical box for John, the haunting Harry Lime theme.

We had eaten our packed lunch on the bus

(I was as bad as the children) and were feeling thirsty. The restaurants were packed with tourists, so we kept walking. 'Can't see any shops along here,' I began, as Katy suddenly decided to descend a flight of steps towards an open door. 'What are you doing?' I called. Maff was close behind her, but he turned and pointed out a notice, before they disappeared from sight.

ALL FRIENDS WELCOME FOR
COFFEE AND CAKES.
SAY FAREWELL TO THE
OLD DOCTOR.

Oh, no, I thought, they don't mean *us!* I entered the portals. I guessed that this was the waiting room off what had been the doctor's surgery. There were tables and chairs, balloons, and the Guest of Honour, opening his gifts at the top table. My children were already seated, and beckoning to me. 'Come on, Mum, we've told the lady you prefer tea, and that we're not allowed coffee!' No-one seemed to mind that we were strangers at the party. The helpers were all smiling. They had made me tea instead of coffee: 'Oh, no trouble, dear!' The cakes were mouth-watering and the children had long glasses of iced lemonade. It was cool in that room and we were grateful for the rest: cobbled streets are hard on the feet.

We slipped away after the speeches, whispered our thanks to the lady in charge, and ran to catch the bus home. Downhill, thank goodness, so we made it just in time.

In a year or two, there was a similar incident far from Kent, but that's another story.

Nine

The Bash Street Lot

Our W.I. had long standing links with an East End settlement. Every summer a coach-load of Londoners arrived at the village hall for a summer treat. Our President, Beatrice, referred to them irreverently as The Bash Street Lot. I soon learned why.

Mrs B had organised the meal. We all contributed to this. We lesser mortals made the tables look pretty with starched cloths, paper napkins and vases of flowers. The welcome party waited at the hall gate in the garden. We all had our appointed tasks, loo patrol, not easy, when they all wanted to go at once; seating guests, or offering a glass of sherry. We were also looking forward to the entertainment which Meg and Millicent had arranged. This had been voted on by the committee, of course. On this occasion Millicent was supplanted at the piano by a distinguished looking man who had a vast repertoire of old-time tunes. We also had a puppeteer as the main attraction. Unfortunately, none of us had seen this chap in action, just been impressed by the fulsome literature sent out by his agent, claiming 'Of TV and radio fame.' Perhaps *radio* was in small letters because how can puppets be presented in that medium? The older ones amongst us had the answer – 'What about Archie Andrews? Peter Brough's naughty schoolboy, was very popular on the wireless in his time. Wasn't he in a programme with Petula Clark?'

After the sherry, lunch was served. It was a cold collation, ham, chicken drumsticks, slices of pork pie, and buttered new potatoes. There were giant bowls of fresh salad, pots of homemade chutney, potato salad, and, unfortunately crisps. Most of the latter crunched noisily underfoot – the hall caretaker would not be amused. There were also baskets of bread rolls. Another mistake.

I was beckoned by a very old man in a fair-isle pullover. 'Ain't you got no sliced bread, love? 'ow am I supposed to eat them rolls with no teeth?' An echo of 'no teeth', went round the table. As most appeared to have a full set, false or otherwise, when they arrived, we guessed that dentures were now in pockets or handbags, wrapped in the dainty paper napkins we'd provided.

'I came prepared,' Mrs B said calmly, when flustered, I ran to her kitchen for help. 'Just in case they wanted sandwiches for tea.' She produced a *Mace* cut loaf from under the counter. By the time 1 got back to my waitress duty, the bread rolls were doing just that, being rolled across the table by several of the Bash Street 'boys.' Also, the little dishes of butter were empty – applied to the already glistening potatoes, or eaten with a spoon, I suspected. Back I ran to the kitchen for the Flora, which had been intended for the sandwiches. They dug enthusiastically with their dinner knives into the big tub of margarine.

'It'll just be strawberries and cream for tea,' Mrs B warned us. 'They had the fairy cakes with the sherry, said they left home before breakfast. That sherry is responsible for the boys. Beer would have been better.'

The Bash street 'girls', in their best frocks, with newly set hair, were merely flushed from the sherry, and very appreciative of all our efforts. 'Lovely ham, dearie. You done us proud. Sorry about the lads – can't take 'em anywhere, eh? Worse'n than kids!'

The pianist had been playing gentle back-ground music all through the lunch hour, and I recall his pleasant tenor voice singing 'I'll be seeing you, in all the old familiar places...' All the chairs were now assembled at the other end of the hall, so that he could continue to entertain the visitors while we dealt with the mess left behind on top of and under the tables and 'cleared the decks' for the puppet show.

I have to commend the Bash Street 'girls'

again, they chattered a lot, but they didn't get up to mischief like the 'boys.' They sang along to all the tunes. They put their teeth back in, too. The boys were restless, and then one called out ''ow about requests?'

The pianist looked apprehensive. 'By all means.' He had discarded his dinner jacket, and poor chap, his shirt was damp with sweat. Rivulets ran down his cheeks from his forehead, as he couldn't pause to mop his head with his handkerchief.

There followed the most ribald songs I had ever not heard, if that makes sense. Most of the W.I. retreated to the kitchen, where we fell about laughing. There were one or two murmurs of 'disgusting,' but I saw that Boffy was tapping her stick in time.

Our Pianist called it a day and departed. The puppets, I'm sorry to say, were just as naughty as the Bash Street males. We didn't know what to do, except smile weakly, and pray it would not be a long ordeal. It was a very saucy show indeed. The Entertainer retorted later, when we told him off, 'I only gave them what they expected. They loved it.' Well, we had no answer to that.

They grumbled about the strawberries. 'We had 'em yesterday, on another outing. We're not supposed to have real cream, clogs you up.' We looked at each other. What about all that farm butter?

'Hurry up with the teapot, Missus,' they called to Mrs B. 'We're going on somewhere else after this, for a fish and chip supper!.' First there were long queues for the loos ... tea is obviously unwise immediately before a journey.

That was the last straw. Meg had a suggestion. 'Next year, let's have the disabled youngsters from my nephew's special school here for a day – we can take them to the farm, visit the donkey sanctuary maybe, play games and have a picnic – what d'you say?'

We said 'Yes!'

The W.I. accounted for most of my social life in those days. Every one of those ladies was special in their own way. They were all my friends, I can't mention them every one by name, but I specially appreciated Boffy, Meg, Millicent, Judy, Eileen from the Mill Cottage (more of her later!) and a newer member Pam, who had moved next door to Beatrice.

Pam was now treasurer (she would later become secretary) of the W.I. We had a special bond because Pam as a toddler had been trapped in her pram by a runaway lorry which had mounted the pavement. Fortunately, Pam had no personal recollection of this event, but it had blighted her mother's life. She had been overprotective of her only child. Pam's father (she obviously inherited her sense of humour and fun from him) was a naval captain. Pam had cared for both parents in their nineties, and had to wait to marry until she was in her mid-thirties. She brewed what she called 'naval tea' – very dark and strong – for her friends, and we listened entranced to her stories of being a magician's assistant and 'sawn in half' on occasion at Toc H shows.

A talking point in Pam's house was a wonderful carved ebony statuette on the banister of the stairs which went up from the hall. This had been fashioned by her father while on a long voyage and presented to her mother. It was a magnificent specimen of a male nude. The captain had been forced by his shocked wife to provide his work with a loin cloth.

The captain had also made a chiming clock, which chimed off-key, part of its charm. His ceremonial sword was fixed to the wall, and was the first thing you saw when you entered the house. Pam's husband had a similar dry humour to his late father in law. Pam was a feisty lady and she and her beloved often had spirited discussions but they were a really devoted couple. Sadly, she was widowed just a few years after they had set up home for the first time on their own. They had no family so generously asked Boffy to join them every Christmas, as she had no close family either.

Later, Pam herself was 'adopted' by a neighbouring young couple. They look after her to this day, now she is very frail. Hilary, whom Pam looks on as a daughter, told me that Pam, who has suffered a stroke and is in a nursing home, said one day, 'I wish I could manage to visit my dear friend Sheila...' I was very touched by that.

W.I. members volunteered to give the vote of thanks to the speaker. One memorable occasion was when Boffy decided she had a very special reason to do so. Our speaker had been with the Metropolitan Police before retiring to this area. He told of us his London beat when he was a young Bobby and of Lord Mayors' Processions and Royal occasions. Boffy was obviously eager to say something at the end. After all, she had been a courier on a tourist bus in London after she retired from her high-powered job doing the same, only abroad. She'd talked to the group about those days.

Question time, and this proved very lively. Then Boffy rose and addressed the speaker in her carrying voice. 'I imagine,' she said, 'This is the first time you have received a vote of thanks from the daughter of a woman who went to prison for assaulting a police officer. She knocked off his helmet with this,' she brandished her stick.

'Er, no,' muttered the ex-policeman. The stick was waved in his direction, and he shifted his position, for he was within striking distance.

To our relief, Boffy continued: 'My mother was of course a suffragette. She was on hunger strike in Holloway and force fed. Unfortunately, I was only a child and couldn't join her, but my sister did. I am very proud of them both.'

'So you should be,' the speaker said fervently. He looked at his watch. 'Would you excuse me – I promised my wife I would be back home by ten. You have been a lovely audience. Thank you.'

The applause was deafening, very gratifying for the speaker, but it was also meant for dear Boffy.

Ten

On the Leslie 'Gateau' trail

1980 was a great year – our first grandchild was born in March, a little red-haired boy, named Matthew after his youthful uncle, so, naturally he was soon known as 'Little Maff.' We visited JP and Di in their new home near Banbury, where JP was stockman on a dairy farm. We were all thrilled to bits with the new member of the family. He slept in a rocking cradle which had been used by generations of our family. They also had two dogs by now, an Old English named Elsa and a Collie Cross Lab, Leo, both very good with the baby. Di and JP's favourite film was, of course, *Born Free.*

This was also the year I became a Romantic Novelist! I was a runner-up in a short story competition, *Friday's Child* was published and I earned the grand sum of £10! I continued with my family anecdotes in magazines, and children's stories, but soon I was writing regularly for *Woman's Realm* – a magazine full of super stories each week – I was thrilled to be among their authors! It was the *Realm's* fiction editor who urged me to write my first novel: that one was seven years in gestation, but the books have flowed, one a year ever since...

Ginge was in her last year at college and itching to see more of the world like her elder sisters, both of whom were already seasoned travellers. The previous summer, Jo went to Israel to work as an au pair for a few months, and, later, to a Kibbutz. She travelled on her own, which worried us, but she proved up to the challenge. However, we were very thankful when Nigel, (soon to be her husband) joined her there, and brought her safely home, just in time to help us celebrate our Silver Wedding. Sara's water-colours were a map of her artistic ventures far afield, too, but she always travelled with a group of friends. When she brought any of these fellow students home, Katy and Maff always seemed to have fits of the giggles as they listened in to earnest conversations, and had to reprimanded. Sara said crossly: 'Mum, they are – *gooseberries!*' Though, Jo found Katy useful in pulling off her tight boots, even if the poor child was propelled backwards across the room clutching the boot, and red-faced from the exertion.

This summer, Jo, who had been temping meanwhile, and living at home, was off again to work on a summer camp in the States!

The boys had already been on holiday, camping in Wales, cheerfully pushing the old banger (the one which was passed down the line for several years, and changed colour frequently) up every minor hill they came to. John and I were missing the earlier family camping trips we had so enjoyed, forgetting all the drawbacks of thistle thick fields and sheer cliff tops, cold showers, getting bogged down in foul-smelling ditches and shivering in the early morning dew; mislaying the pegs so that the tent had 'lift off' in a bitter wind. We recalled lovely sunny days, the smell of bacon and eggs as John stood over the little cooker in the back of the mini-bus.

'Let's have an adventure,' John said. 'You, me and the young ones. We'll look out for a second-hand caravan and go to Scotland – to where I was as a boy during the war.'

We were enthusiastic, having been en-thralled by all his stories over the years, especially those about his friend Leslie Catto – a name converted to 'Gateau', by the children – whom he hoped to see again.

We acquired a Sprite four-berth caravan, a veteran it's true, but just what we were looking for – still sound, and although basic inside, compared with today's splendid mobile homes, comfortable. We could tell it had been well looked after by previous owners. We enjoyed buying pots and pans, gas cylinders, a hammock bed for Maff to go over Katy's single bunk, a portaloo with a large container of 'blue', a water carrier and new sleeping bags. We added a battery radio and serviced the fridge. John fitted a tow bar to the car. He had a practice run or two; we planned our trip to take in places of interest and were ready to go the last week in August. Ginge would be home to oversee the boys and look after Billow. The latter, of course, was a doddle, compared to the former! Though, Michael and Roger had their bantams to see to.

Katy and Maff were just the right age for this venture; she would be off to the comprehensive school in September. She was now an enthusiastic Girl Guide, although as she was so petite she wore her blue blouse as a dress, with a belt round it and didn't need a skirt! She could have tucked her long golden hair in the belt, we said. Maff, now boyishly short-haired but still with the white flash on his crown, which had given him the alternative family name of 'Plume', didn't take to the Scouts, unlike his brothers before him – Jonathan had difficulty at the end to find a spare inch of shirt to sew on all his badges!

But both Maff and Katy loved the outdoor life. They explored all the country lanes round us. Katy was small and light enough to ride a friend's Shetland pony but Maff cycled alongside her, to make sure she was safe. He is still a very caring chap. His main hobby then was his two pet goats, which he kept in a local field. We benefited from the milking later – except for the time they unwisely ingested bulrushes...

As in the past, we couldn't wait until the Saturday morning to set off on our epic journey. We left on the Friday, early evening, planning to make our first stop before dark. We didn't reach a camping site before dusk. After we came off the motorway, we made for a service station on the outskirts of Birmingham, only to find the car park too full to accommodate the caravan, so we had no alternative but to spend the night in the lorry park! It was quite unnerving, parked in the midst of all those giant articulated vehicles.

We lit the gas lamps in the caravan. Pulled the curtains. At least we had plenty of food and water, and most importantly, a loo in a cubbyhole. The kettle hissed on the little stove and I asked Katy to pass the teapot.

'You forgot to bring it Mum!' she told me.

'You know I can't stand teabags,' John said unreasonably.

I thought it wise not to admit I hadn't any loose-leaf tea either...

I'll draw a veil over the roar of engines and loud voices, as lorries departed before dawn. We were on our way too, as soon as it was light, after I dunked the tea bags in mugs, but no-one said a word.

I'm a bad traveller, though unfortunately for John I can sleep when I should be navigating, though this annoying habit of mine can be a boon. It's a relief if I can manage to snooze away many miles of motorway, but I do endeavour to keep awake along the scenic routes.

'Thank goodness!' John said, with feeling, after we'd driven through the Cheviots, and I perked up, eyes open at last, feeling thoroughly refreshed. 'We've been on a regular switchback ride – I thought the caravan would jack-knife! "Don't you two dare wake Mum!" I said.'

The second afternoon we arrived at Loch Ness. It was a gloomy spot, with looming trees, unexpectedly deserted. While I rustled up refreshments, the children amused themselves and let off steam by rolling and whooping down a grassy bank. 'You'll frighten the sheep,' John said. The sheep were significant, as you will see, later. We made up our minds to travel on to a camping site a few miles on. Both Katy and I felt too nervous to stay where we were, in case the monster reared its ugly head. I don't think that Maff and John were too keen either, otherwise why didn't they try to persuade us to stay there?

The camp site was a very superior one, expensive, too, owned by a Lord, no less. There were rules and regulations and we were chided for not belonging to the Caravan Club. (We joined the next season.) Here John ran the car battery flat by connecting the radio. While he charged the battery, we enjoyed the luxury of hot showers, despite the warning: *You Will Be Prosecuted If You Steal The Towels.*

I privately thought you wouldn't be tempted to do any such thing, because the towels were worn and skimpy. We were still damp and needed to struggle back into our clothes.

This was a working farm, and we enjoyed fresh milk and eggs from the little shop. Top prices. Aristocratic hens and cows, we decided.

On we travelled, and at last reached our destination. John's wartime journey as a small boy with his family by train had been very different to ours. They had boarded the train during an air-raid at King's Cross. Stirred by the story, I later wrote *The Spirit of Millie Mae* (Hale). I will let you into a secret ... the young boy in my book, Barney Rainbow, is based on the character of John, and the setting in Scotland is the very same fishing village.

We had driven along the coastal road with tantalising glimpses of the glistening sea and stretches of silvery sand below towering cliffs. The old railway track for local freight which John remembered had gone: in its place was a small private caravan park. It was just a few steps over a track to the beach, a perfect site for a holiday.

The next morning we were impatient to climb the steep street with grey stone and slate cottages which overlooked the harbour, to find the place where John and his sisters and his parents had stayed during the middle years of the war. John's Dad was a contracts manager for the building of new runways at the aerodrome at Lossiemouth, and where he went, so did his family. His two older sisters had just left school and secretarial college and took jobs in Elgin, the nearest town. John and his younger sister Pam went to the local school and endured some tough times. There were a couple of other boys who were not local so they stuck together and stood up to the real bullies. The head teacher was very stern and the tawse, a strap, was often employed for minor misdemeanours.

John sniffed the air: 'There was always an all pervading smell of fish soup then – our landlady cooked fish for us most days! I used to go with the local boys in the late afternoon and watch the fishermen sorting their catch. All the children except for my friend Leslie, the Minister's son, spoke Gaelic when out of school. We stood back from the crowd, not fitting in.' He conjured up for us the black clad women, knitting busily with one hand, with the second needle thrust in their belts, as the fishermen threw the undersized cod and herring to the boys. The test was to see which one could achieve the longest string of tiny silver fish, as the lads threaded them through the gills.

'I learned how to prepare them for my mum, by watching the younger women gutting them with their sharp knives, quick as lightning, they were. As their fingers were all scaley and fishy, they only ate the middle of their jam sandwiches.'

'Is that all they had?' asked Katy in disbelief: '*Jam* in their sandwiches?'

'Yes, so did *we* often during the war!' John and I agreed.

We went downhill to the harbour but there were no fishermen or boats to be seen, nor young lassies gutting fish. The smoking huts were deserted. The rainbow hued combinations, all-in-one undergarments, knitted by the grannies from scraps of wool, which kept their men folk warm in bad weather, no longer fluttered on the washing lines. That was a disappointment, too.

However, it was still a fascinating place. The soft sand stretched for miles. Cormorants zoomed low over our heads as we walked along, and pigeons and herring gulls chattered and swore in the clefts in the sandstone rocks. The children paused at the rock pools, exclaiming over the hermit crabs in their protective whelk shells which disappeared under the trails of glossy, green seaweed. We came at last to the blow-hole, a huge rock with a hole in the centre. The sea rushed furiously at the rock, just as John had said it would, the spray smacked our faces as we stood gazing at the spectacle as the water burst through the blow hole with a roar like thunder. It was awesome and exhilarating.

There was a bakery where we purchased soft baps and lardy cakes for our daily picnics. We were on the Leslie Gateau trail, and he was very elusive. The assistant in the shop remembered his family. 'Aye, they moved on when the Minister retired. I heard they went to Edinburgh... Young Leslie became a doctor, they say.'

We needed to adjust our mental picture of Young Leslie. John's memory was of a lively boy, the youngest of four brothers, who'd told his friend, 'If you have a good wash at nights, you don't need to bother in the mornings!' (John's mum didn't agree with this theory!) They'd had great fun cycling in and out of a box-hedge maze in the manse garden. We all wanted to meet Leslie, but

Edinburgh ... the festival was on, and it seemed impossible. I think I must tell you now, that we haven't found him yet. Does anyone out there know Leslie *Catto*?

It was lovely weather, and one day, when Katy was wearing a brief sun top, Maff observed: 'You've grown a jelly mole on your back, Kate!' She tried to see it, but couldn't and I was called to give an opinion on this phenomenon. 'Ugh!' I cried, 'You've got a horrible *tick* on you!' We'd had to deal with these on Billow before now. John said she must have got it when she rolled down-hill among the sheep at Loch Ness.

The nearest doctor we were told, was at the next village along the coast. We drove over there immediately. A friendly local directed us to the surgery: 'The house behind the yellow car, see?'

The door was open, and Katy and I ventured shyly inside. The waiting room was an ordinary sitting room and there was only one elderly lady in a wheelchair waiting her turn. We sat down beside her, and she seemed pleased to see us and talked a lot, although we couldn't understand everything she said. Half an hour went by, then I asked her: 'Isn't the doctor here yet?'

Our companion laughed. 'Oh, this isn't the doctor's house. That's two doors further up! This is my house, but I'm glad to have met you.'

We hurried along to the surgery. Another open door into a sitting room. It was full of patients, who stared at us then ignored us. I heard one say to another, 'Tis the visitors that gave us this terrible cough...' We kept quiet in case they pointed an accusing finger. Prominent in the room was a piano. There was a large notice propped on top. It read: *Will Patients Kindly Refrain From Playing The Piano.*

'Oh blow!' whispered a disappointed voice in my ear. 'Shush!' I warned young Katy.

When it was our turn, she jumped up on the couch, still wearing her little red wellies, which she said were a protection against jelly fish when paddling. The young bearded doctor was a ringer for Doctor Finlay (as in his casebook) and just as charming. He tweezed out the horrible tick while telling us a lighted cigarette was quicker, while not recommended. Relieved of the jelly mole, Katy danced out of the surgery, all smiles.

Maff and John wanted to know where on earth we had been. This was a wonderful holiday and we enjoyed almost every moment (except for the tick, of course.) On our way home we went to the airport to collect Jo, and heard of her travels on the Greyhound Buses.

Eleven

A Family crisis, followed by Two Summer Weddings

The late night phone call from JP had us reeling with shock; our dear little grandson was critically ill in hospital. He'd seemed off colour, that was all, but after Jonathan had gone to work that morning, the baby had turned blue and become unconscious. A neighbour summoned an ambulance and Di went with him to the hospital – neither of them would return home for several weeks. Young Matthew was not yet two years old, and Di was pregnant with their second baby.

An emergency operation revealed that from birth one of his kidneys had been unable to function properly because of stenosis; the baby had been poisoned by the build-up of toxins unable to escape in the normal way. It really was touch-and-go, and the little boy was in intensive care for some time.

At last we had good news – they were coming home! We drove the long miles between us to see them reunited. That small chap was actually bouncing about and laughing, when we walked into their living room, but I shall never forget poor Di's pale, wan face and her obvious exhaustion.

Throughout his childhood, young Matthew was often in hospital, for smaller operations, but has always been serene and positive. He is in his twenties now and keeps fit and healthy, enjoying rock-climbing, so there was a happy outcome. He has always been studious, and deserves the success he enjoys in his working life. We salute you, Matt!

Two weddings, two weeks apart – we took it in our stride! Two wedding cakes, one with yellow ribbons, the other with pink. The first to be married were Ginge and Allen. She had been working in Denmark for a year, caring for a small boy – this was after a short period as one of a team of carers for quins born in Kent! She'd met Allen at college, and he was already teaching. The children in his class called him McEnroe, because of his similar hairstyle – however, he had – has – a sunny laid-back temperament, and plays drums in a local band! As for sport, one of his wry stories was of being a marshal in a cross-country race and somehow directing the runners in the wrong direction! Well, he was engrossed in a book at the time, was his excuse.

Their reception was held in the half-acre garden at Allen's parents' house in a village near Sittingbourne. We helped to clean an old barn and set up trestles for the wedding breakfast. John and Jack, Allen's Dad, donned striped aprons and carved turkey and ham with aplomb. It was a beautiful day, we sat in the garden soaking up the sun and even cut the cake out there. It was all very relaxed and it was definitely an occasion to store in the memory.

Sara fashioned beautiful fragrant bouquets for her sisters, to match their dresses, in turn. She picked the flowers from Allen's parents' garden for Virginia, who wore a floaty, Indian cotton frock in pinks and purples: with her long, dark hair and sandals she was the perfect outdoors bride. Allen, who is not one for suits, but feels (and looks) right in comfortable casual clothes, borrowed a grey suit from his dad! Young relatives, including little Maff, climbed trees and older ones relaxed – we still had speeches and toasts to bride and groom, but the informality of it all was great.

Katy was bridesmaid, and repeated her role a fortnight later for Jo and Nigel, who were married in our local church. They had been sweethearts since they were at school. Jo wore a jade green silk dress, and in the centre of her posy was a perfect peach coloured rose from the chapel garden. This has been known as Joanna's rose, ever since.

Michael, being the proud owner of a new white mini, provided the wedding car for the bride, his little sister and their father. It was a ten-minute walk to the church, so most of the other guests went ahead, to join the groom and the best man. Nigel's mum, Mary and I thought we were being collected later, but as time went on, we decided we'd have to make a run for it, to be there on time! We needed to be speedy, for it had begun to rain. Panting, we arrived, just before the bride, who had been touring round until everyone was safety in the church! I guess we looked a bit bedraggled, but then, all eyes were on the bride!

It was unexpected when our dear Jo walked down the aisle to the strains of *All Things Bright and Beautiful* – difficult to match your steps to, as she said later, but it was her favourite hymn. Katy, naturally, skipped behind the bride and her father.

This time there was a thunderstorm and there was a power cut, so the organ ceased in our mid-hymn singing. We rushed back to the chapel for the party, where John, thinking everyone would need a cup of tea, brewed it in the caravan in the drive! He remarked ruefully, 'I didn't think about the wine glasses lined up at the ready!' He was soon busy carving yet another turkey and ham, and I put out proudly the big bowls of special trifle, just as I had on our Silver Wedding Day.

Another very happy time, with extended family and old friends congratulating the newlyweds. Both girls had requested simple, family weddings, and were very contented with their lot.

Following the weddings, we had visitors from America. Mollie and Laurance were cousins of my mother. Mollie's father had emigrated to Canada in 1910 to a place called Moose Jaw. Mollie's mother sang in the church choir (she was from Lancashire) and they met and married there. He built his own wooden house, he'd trained as a carpenter on a big estate in Suffolk. Times were tough, conditions primitive, but the pioneers thrived, as their family grew. Eventually they moved on to North Dakota, where Great Uncle Joe became a wealthy man.

We had already met Mollie's lively sister Jean a year before, when she embarked on a whirlwind tour of 'the old country.' She and Katy immediately bonded, as they were alike in many ways, small, and live wires! Jean had obviously been the Katy of her day! Maff and Katy stuck to Jean like glue, and reported to us: 'Jean has what she calls a *bosom buddy* – it's her wallet and she buttons it up inside the front of her blouse!' I can picture them giggling when Jean, who had unwisely taken them shopping, had to unbutton herself to extract a traveller's cheque! We took Jean to Ellen Terry's Cottage, at Smallhythe, and she couldn't resist touching things, which alarmed the custodian, 'just think, the great actress must have loved this – or that–' she cried, in her excitement. I almost felt like pretending I wasn't with her and my children!

Mollie was tall and beautiful, and much quieter. Laurance was the ebullient one of the two. They were over here for a year, renting a tiny cottage at Sevenoaks. They were recently retired from teaching English and music. Both had lovely singing voices.

That year, during Christmas week we invited them to join us at our local church to listen to the Canterbury Singers who were in concert there. It was a chilly evening, but we wrapped up warmly and stepped out smartly together to the church. Bells rang to welcome us inside. Latecomers reported, 'It's beginning to snow!' We sang all the lovely old carols, and enjoyed the anthems by the visiting singers. John's cousin was among them. There was a bird fluttering above the choir's heads, disturbing their concentration. The verger attempted to prop open an overhead window to allow the bird to escape. What happened next was that snow poured in through the window, which

147

the verger was unable to close, and cascaded down the necks of the unfortunate singers. To their credit, apart from the initial gasps of surprise, they carried on with their repertoire. In the front pews, we were now all shivering with cold, too.

However, when we came out of the church and found a white world, it just added to a magical evening. We linked arms and trudged back to the chapel singing: 'Show me the way to go home'. Our relatives were worried about driving back to Sevenoaks in a snowstorm, so we set to, to make up spare beds and moved family around.

Mollie often reminded me of that happy evening, and the giant dish of macaroni cheese we conjured up for supper, followed by a large treacle tart! Simple things taste good at such times, don't they?

During the Christmas break, Katy and Maff went to stay with them for a few days – again it snowed, and they had to journey home by train. We didn't worry, because dear Maff was so sensible and looked after his big (little) sister... Katy came home in a new warm dress, run-up from a tartan curtain by clever Mollie – well, she was the daughter of a pioneer! She'd learned to sew as a child when her mother boiled up sugar sacks and Mollie joined a group of church-women who made (beautifully embroidered) muslin nightgowns for babies, pillowcases, and other useful items. Jean was given a pair of tea towels when she married Del sixty years ago, which she treasures in her memory box.

Each December, we festoon our tree with white frosted lights which Mollie and Laurance brought with them from America and then gave to us, when they returned home. They both passed away recently, but my latest book *The Watercress Girls* was inspired by the five Mackley girls, as they were known, and I'm glad Mollie knew I had written 'their story'. Jean, the younger sister, helped greatly with the research of this novel.

Twelve

Well, There's kids – and kids...

'Would you come and help with reading at school?' Meg asked me. I guess she thought it was about time I had a new challenge. I'm not sure she approved of me typing furiously away at my stories on the dining room table. That was too introspective in her view.

So I spent afternoons with Meg's juniors and it took me back to when I was ten years old and along with a couple of other children was given the task of coaching slow-readers for the term before they went to secondary school. Only recently, my old friend Anne, who had been a fellow pupil-teacher, told me of the shock she'd felt when she learned that the boy she had helped, was killed when a flying-bomb hit his house. She never spoke of it, at the time.

The books were more lively and entertaining than they had been then. It was good to see the children growing in confidence, and fluent in reading aloud.

There was a new headmaster, and one day he had a request, too. Would I read to a group of children in his study for an hour on Friday afternoons? These were children who often disrupted the quiet reading sessions which all the teachers took in turn; they fidgeted and annoyed the better behaved. This was a challenge indeed! Was I up to it?

I sat within the circle of nine and ten year olds, more boys than girls, and opened the Puffin book with some trepidation. One of the girls was shifting about in her seat, and held out her hand. 'Look Miss, I got an engagement ring in Play today. D'you think he got it out of a cracker?'

'Very nice,' I said lamely, ignoring the question, in case the boy concerned was offended. Then I took a deep breath and began reading that wonderful children's classic, *The Silver Sword* by Ian Serrailler. It was a book which Virginia, I recalled, had loved at this age. But these were not avid readers, they were restless, they would rather be outside, kicking a football around. This was the story of three young Polish children, two sisters and a brother, refugees during WW2, who travel across Europe to find their missing father. He has escaped from prison and made his way back, to find his home in Warsaw in ruins and his children gone. Jan, an orphaned lad, befriends the family and this resourceful boy helps them to survive and to be reunited eventually with their father.

I read on and on, as absorbed in the story as the children. They sat quiet as mice, and listened. I didn't hear the bell announcing time to go home, neither did they. Had I really been reading aloud for an hour?

The headmaster looked in at us. He smiled. 'Did you enjoy the story, children?'

A concerted chorus of 'Yes, Sir!'

They were not the only ones who went

home with their head in the clouds.

Some time later, there was a vacancy for a dinner lady, and I was asked to apply for the job. Matt (he preferred that now to Maff) had joined Kate (she preferred that to Katy) at the senior school, told me the school dinners at the old school were great – and that convinced me! A free dinner was part of the deal. The hours were from eleven a.m. until two p.m. – we had our lunch, served the children, then went into the school field or playground to supervise them, while the teachers had a well-earned break. After a few months, another helper and myself were asked to be classroom assistants for an hour in the afternoons, which we both enjoyed. The meals were indeed very good, for the school cook was the daughter of a London chef who had taught her to cook when she was young.

I am now going to dip into *My Weekly* magazine again to catch the flavour of what happened one day while I was at the school 'on field duty.' The article was entitled, 'I'm

Frightened to Guess Who's Coming To Dinner!' The magazine commented: 'There's something different served up every day...' True words, indeed. They were written in the present tense, and do you know, it still feels like that, all these years later!

As I turn the corner and hurry down Church hill towards our little Victorian village school, my mouth begins to water.

To me, who so dreaded school dinners as a child, the aromas wafting from the kitchen are heavenly. I remember, with a little shiver, those loathsome, dark green greens and the Terrible Twins who would 'oblige' – for a price – with my pud! We had ledges beneath our trestle tables where lurked little paper bags, grease spotted with gristle, waiting to be furtively removed and planted in the school garden. We were 'digging for victory' then, and I suspect the teachers added their contributions, too!

'Hello, Sheila,' says Clare, our cheerful cook. She has performed wonders with the temperamental old cooker as usual and when we've got the kettle on, filled the water jugs and set the trolley, we sit down to our lunch at 11.30 a.m.

Zoe, my fellow dinner lady, takes a peek at the sweets. Whatever shall we have? Every day there's something tempting – and often celebratory. The whole school clapped the Easter gateaux!

'I've made some meringue nests – they freeze well, Clare tells us. I'll fill them with fresh strawberries, do you think the children will approve?'

'Oh yes, and so will we!'

Health-conscious parents need not worry now. School dinners are delicious, nutritious and well balanced. Clare uses wholemeal flour and not too much fat. Fresh fruit and crisp salads figure prominently in the menus.

Replete, Zoe and I trundle the trolleys into the adjoining hall. This lofty, once grim and depressing room has been transformed by the energetic staff with the help of parents.

White walls and lipstick-red paintwork are embellished with the children's colourful and imaginative paintings and poems. We move in smart rhythm down the length of the hall, clattering knives and forks into position, placing water jugs, salt and pepper pots, plastic beakers and chairs for the staff.

As Clare unplugs the heated trolley in the kitchen, the first children come eagerly in.

'What's for lunch today?'

To me: 'I like your shoes – the man who lives in our house has got a pair the same!' (Dubious compliment, don't you agree?)

'Tell him off! He pulled my jumper!'

'Did you watch the horror film last night?' No, I was in bed asleep!

'My mum had a new baby in the middle of the night. When I woke up my granny was there and she told me.'

'I got two house-points for my story – look, it's on the wall.'

'I put a sheep's skull on the nature table. My teacher was very surprised.' (I bet she was.)

'I don't want any dinner – sniff! I've got a tummy-ache.'

'Look at my fingers! My brother done it.' (Pulls back plaster to reveal miniscule injury.)

The children settle down, and hands are demurely folded, eyes downcast (except for Terry's) as the teacher on duty leads The Grace.

Today it's my turn to help dish-up. Zoe pours water, cuts up the little ones' food, listens to the latest news, and keeps an eye generally on the children.

Normal – Medium – Spot are the menu sizes, but now and again, a large, hungry child will request, 'Gigantic, please!' or a nervous newcomer will whisper, 'Do I have to have any?' We encourage them to 'have just a little' which is invariably tried and eaten. Soon hands are shooting up eagerly for seconds. The 'Custard King' has been known to consume four platefuls!

Zoe is first out in the playground with the children. In winter we feel restricted as balls

157

whizz around our heads, marbles are disputed and every tumble necessitates first-aid.

Boys disappear round the shed, crawl under the mobile classroom, climb on to the oil-tank wall. Girls tend to creep back indoors to lurk in the toilets, or join forces with those legitimately pasting and cutting for the babies' class.

There is the occasional joy of snowballs – provided you've brought your wellies – but how we long for the weather to improve so we can have a Field Day!

The large school field rolls and rollicks downhill and the views of farmland, trees and church are magnificent. The football pitch and running tracks are marked in the spring and our teams soon become used to the vagaries of the turf.

Today, cartwheels, handstands and headstands are practised on the springy grass. Little boys make clouds of dust fly in the ditches as they zoom their model cars, and Zoe and I are soon clutching bunches of daisies and clover. Our pockets bulge with discarded recorders and dolls as we keep a watchful eye on the far corners.

A cluster of boys looks suspicious. I wander down to take a look. Do they, like me at that age, have secret bags of food to dispose of?

'Watch out! He'll bite you!' I hear.

I quicken my pace. Little Jenny had mentioned a snake to us yesterday. Probably a worm, we'd thought – or a figment of her fertile mind. Am I seeing things, or is that a *goat?*

It is! Lydia has her arm slung familiarly round its neck. The bearded mouth snaffles the last crisps and its tail swishes with pleasure.

'Look! Isn't he lovely? He must have got through the hedge!' Or was he enticed?

'She,' I correct her, thinking ... I recognise that goat ... it's either Lucy or Drusy – my son Matt keeps her in the farm field beyond.

Zoe and I examine the hole in the hedge. 'That's where that awful Barnaby escaped last year, d'you remember? It was the last day of term. When he got found out, he said we'd given him permission.'

Lucy/Drusy doesn't want to return that way – in fact she won't budge. She likes the children, she likes the cuddles – and she's nosing in pockets for more tit-bits.

I sprint back to the school. 'Help!' I cry to a passing teacher. She finds a long coil of rope.

It's easy enough to catch a docile goat and to thread rope through its collar, but it takes the whole football team to urge her up the field. Then she clatters crossly across the asphalt, has an inspection of the staff's cars and reluctantly accompanies me back to the farm. The children are very disappointed to see her go.

It's a hot day and I'm perspiring. I thought our old dog pulled, but he's nothing compared to this goat.

Luckily for him, Matt is not about! I pen the goat up. Then– Where's the other one? Drusy/Lucy has vanished, too!

I hack my way through the nettles and thistle towards the dividing hedge. There's the hole – and there's Drusy/Lucy investigating its possibilities egged on by the children on the other side.

Drusy/Lucy is not as friendly as her sister. She shows her teeth at me and kicks my already nettle-stung ankle. I hop back, hand through her collar, chanting endearments, but thinking blue murder. As I give her a helping hand into the pen, I hear the whistle.

I stagger back uphill and puff along the playground. The children, filing back inside the school, greet me excitedly.

'Cor, your face is all red!'

'Can't you bring the goats in to play tomorrow?'

'Aren't you lucky having goats in your family!'

I smile weakly. Wait until I see my son tonight!

We supervise the babies in the washrooms and then see them back to their classroom. Like magic, the noise subsides, and they sit

161

quietly on their mat to listen to a story.

I still have a car in my pocket, and the handle of a skipping rope. Clare is washing the floor of the kitchen.

'Had a good lunch-hour?' she asks.

'We've had a *Field Day!*' I say, with feeling.

Thirteen

Putting on our Parts

We were having our W.I. committee meeting at Millicent's house. She lived in an old lodge within a secluded, lovingly tended garden, with her two aged dogs. 'From the same mother, would you believe it,' she said. Well, they certainly didn't look like sisters. The bigger dog, which resembled a golden Labrador, was named Beauty; the tiny, scruffy, whiskery one, was black – no, she wasn't called Beast, for she had a very sweet nature, was the more intelligent of the two, and answered to Tuppence.

Millicent's house was a reflection of her artistic temperament – she was obviously multi-talented. She had been brought up by an eccentric aunt and uncle. She told us stories of her unconventional childhood, how she'd gone along with her aunt to Ellen Terry's cottage where her aunt was hanging new curtains she had made for the actress. Millicent was fascinated by the bed, which was chained to the wall, because of the sloping floor. She thought Miss Terry would have had much more fun careening down the room in it.

Besides being a musician, choir mistress and enthusiastic gardener, Millicent also painted and potted: she constantly took up new crafts, and was busy with several projects at the same time. There were half woven baskets, glowing tapestries folded over chair arms – 'Watch out for the needles!' she reminded us cheerfully. Her pride and joy was a grand piano, with piles of music scores, some of which she had composed herself.

When we had completed the 'business', she bustled into her kitchen, colourful with tiles she had hand-painted, and made a big pot of tea. We enjoyed her buttered scones (she was a good cook, too) and drank tea from bone china cups.

'Let's have a sing-song,' she encouraged us, as the dogs hoovered up our crumbs. She sat down at the piano. We awaited her command.

Unfortunately, our singing upset Beauty, who lifted her head and howled, very loudly indeed. Tuppence joined in with a 'woof' or two. Millicent had arranged us in a circle of chairs around her as she played. The dogs were in the middle of us. Catastrophe! Beauty produced an enormous puddle, which lapped round our feet. Singing faltered and our pianist swivelled round crossly: 'Why have you stopped!' Then she realised that we were all sneakily abandoning ship – well our seats anyway. She sighed, went into the kitchen and came back with a large saucepan and a dish cloth. The more genteel members blanched at the choice of mopping up utensils. Millicent was obviously expert at this task. Poor Beauty hid behind the settee.

'Now you're all here,' Millicent said, surprised that we didn't want a second cup of tea or another scone, 'I have a bright idea... We should put on a village pantomime, as we used to in the old days. Sheila can write it for us, I'll compose some music, and produce it, of course. All agreed? I'll have a casting session here next week.'

So that's how I began my pantomime career – Millicent produced a tattered script. All of three pages, and commanded: 'Enlarge it!' How could I resist *Cinderella?* Before I knew it, I was an Ugly Sister, too. I never revealed that I had written my first pantomime at nine years old in primary school, and also appeared in that as Puss in Boots, in a costume fashioned from our old blackout curtains! Millicent had suspected I was a thwarted actress, and she was right. Mind you, the Sunday school I attended when six or seven had a job to find a Joseph willing to play opposite my Mary in the Nativity play. Eventually, the undertaker's son obliged, but I'm afraid I had to whisper his lines to him. He mumbled a threat or two through his grey woolly beard. Looking back, I guess it was my enthusiasm that put them off. Later, when we studied Shakespeare in English lessons and acted in front of the class, I was Lady Macbeth, 'Out damned spot!' I cried, then I was Shylock – I enjoyed the character parts – I wasn't so keen to play Henry V's Queen. Perhaps it's time to reveal that I was shy and quiet when I was young, but I surprised my family and friends when 'throwing myself' into a part!

Every single member of the W.I. was roped in for that first panto. Judy painted backdrops and designed posters, tickets and the programme. She and Alice made wonderful props, like the coach in which Cinderella went to the Ball, and an enormous pumpkin from vacuum cleaner bags. Molly, Boffy's neighbour, designed 'wings' on stage from old curtains, Boffy advised on costume, of course. Pam sat in the prompt corner. John's sister Betty came up with some lyrics for Millicent's new music, including Cinderella's song – snippet at the beginning of this book!

Millicent arranged the footlights, trained those who didn't wish to act to produce special effects, and produced songs and music which were a challenge to us all. Cinderella, our youngest member, looked the part, but refused to sing. Mrs B, in the wings, provided the voice, pure and sweet, as Cinderella mimed the words. Buttons, on the other hand, could sing, and was a champion tap dancer! I had a great partner in Joan, the guide captain – she was the bossy Ugly Sister and I was the Put-Upon one – we were both after the Prince, but our feet were too big for the glass slipper. All the cast were dedicated, and again I can't mention them all, but one who stole the show was a tiny lady, known ever after as Fairy Maud! Also, there was Eileen, from the Mill cottage. Eileen played a minor role on this occasion, but later she had the plum parts, like Wishee Washee in Aladdin! She was another small, dark haired, slim lady, who had been born in S. Africa and married an Englishman during the war. She loved cats and we heard all about Rhubarb and Custard, the current pair. We also learned that she had a famous daughter, a delightful actress, Linda Bassett, who came with her friends to all our shows, and applauded us enthusiastically from the front row. Linda obviously got her gift for drama from her little mum!

At the dress rehearsal, we were joined by Millicent's quartet. The music made all the difference. 'You don't need a microphone!' Millicent cried to the faint-hearted. 'Just project your voice!' We learned to come front stage and to involve the audience.

Children from the local dancing school, dressed as mice, provided the 'Aah!' element. We wore our costumes for the first time too.

Joan and I had our best moment when we had a tussle on stage. Alice made me a 'pull apart' dress. When Joan grabbed me from behind as I displayed my finery to the audience, she declaimed: 'Your frock does nothing to camouflage flab– That pink

169

makes you look like an overdressed crab!' I was revealed in outsize bloomers and long-sleeved vest. We were expecting laughter from the audience, but to my astonishment, the overwhelming reaction from them, was sympathy for poor downtrodden Aggie. I felt like a born-again actress – it was heart-warming! I realised the audience *liked* me! Linda gave me a hug and said I had missed my vocation! I've been a great fan of hers ever since. I loved her performance in *Lark Rise to Candleford* on T.V.

Year by year, the pantomimes continued, and other groups asked if they might borrow our scripts. Millicent, Meg and I got to see most of these productions! The tickets were invariably a sell-out, and we gave all the money raised to charity. By now, most of us were tap dancing along with 'Buttons.'

In mufti one afternoon, walking along the village street, I was hailed by a passing stranger on a bicycle: 'Why, it's Mother Goose!' I knew then I couldn't hide 'behind my character'!

We also began to tour round residential and nursing homes at Christmas with shorter, slicker versions of the pantomimes – I called these Potted Pantos. Just a few props, and quick changes of costume, and Millicent on the piano. We had an amusing if rueful experience once. We had been invited to another W.I.'s Christmas party, as the entertainment. Millicent previewed the stage and facilities, and told us, 'They have an excellent piano, thank goodness.' What we didn't know was that the 'resident' pianist who had fought long and hard to get that instrument, wasn't about to let us or rather Millicent, loose on it. She got the caretaker to move it to a hiding place behind the stage, and to put the old piano in its place.

We began on a high note, literally, for only the top keys functioned, most of the rest were dumb. Millicent bashed at them furiously, to no effect, and we squeaked our way through the songs. A quick glance at Millicent's quivering back, clad in shiny black

171

satin, made us quake. Afterwards, we bolted down our cake and made for the exit without the usual pleasantries. Millicent never forgot – and certainly never forgave the perpetrator.

So now, rather as I had been in the old days when we were knee deep in plums, I was the village scribe, though then I was writing letters for the gypsies. I wrote for the local paper, for the church magazine and I penned more plays and pantomimes for the school. This reduced the time I could devote to paid writing, but I was still busy with articles on family life and romantic stories set in the past. I wasn't the only one researching and typing at the rate of knots: Marcia and Ian were involved with a book about our village. Judy, Ian's wife produced lots of her delightful pen and ink drawings, an example being a pair of oxen pulling the plough. I was asked to edit the book for them, which meant I had the privilege of reading it before most of the village. It was a labour of love for the three of them and a job well done.

I have told you something of some of the folk I knew then, but there were others with interesting stories which they longed to share. Mostly single, elderly ladies who would surprise and delight us all. I was asked to write a series on Village Voices for the Parish mag. Beatrice, the retired District Nurse had a great deal to tell. She had trained as a Norland Nanny and when she was in college, her father visited her one day. She was told in no uncertain terms that men were not allowed on the premises. 'He's not a suitor, he's my father!' Bea protested. But the rules could not be bent. She became Nanny to a famous film star's family and enjoyed it very much. At the beginning of the war, she retrained as a hospital nurse, and was in London through-out the blitz. There were tales of her early 'district days' – of working in slums but how her impoverished clients always made her a cup of tea, and one dear old man covered each step of the stairs to his flat with old

173

newspapers to protect her shoes, and also placed a paper on the seat of her chair. She remarked that there was dignity in poverty. When a child saw her coming up the stairs with her black bag and exclaimed: 'Blimey, I 'ope you ain't got a new baby in that!' Beatrice opened it to prove she hadn't. 'Just come to cut Grandad's toenails,' she said. She took her guides to Norway on camping holidays, and sewed her money bag to her underwear for safe keeping.

There was another lady of the same vintage who had connections with the film world. She had been engaged at 20 to a young actor. Her father wouldn't allow her to marry him, but Kay followed his career avidly, and was glad he married happily and had a family. She respected her father's wishes, she said, and never contacted him again. She had worked for a well-known firm of cotton thread and embroidery silk manufacturers. Kay was a secretary in the office, but over the years she collected samples of all the colours you could imagine. She embroidered pictures on linen as gifts, from her own designs. Another hobby, besides her real passion, gardening, was writing jingles for greetings cards, and she was very good at this.

These thumbnail sketches, led to me being asked to write tributes to be read at funerals. I also wrote, at his dictation, the life story of an elderly farmer who wanted copies for his family and friends. I called it 'Give him the best, but in a smaller glass', words spoken by his own father, when he was a lad, and allowed his first taste of beer. It needed tweaking and some tactful editing (he'd had two wives and two families!) and it bore his name as author, of course, but he was very pleased with the end result. Extracts were read at his funeral, as he wished. Most of the congregation, including us, had been privileged to attend his 80th birthday celebrations not long before. We all said he had enjoyed every minute of it, and that was a good feeling.

John and I were very proud when we

learned from the farmer's wife that her husband had remarked, when in turn, our sons gained a good grounding working at weekends on the farm, while they were still at school: 'Those boys are a cut over other boys.' This was praise indeed from one who did not give it lightly.

Fourteen

Merv the Midnight Grocer

Marcia and her family were enthusiastic about a wonderful holiday in a narrow boat on the Mon and Brec (Monmouthshire and Brecon) Canal in Wales. 'Why don't you take your children – they'd love it! The dog, too.'

Kate and Matt were teenagers now, and they thought it was a great idea. We arrived at Gilwern, at the offices of the Princess Line, and were taken aboard to learn the ropes.

The long boat was traditionally decorated with larger than life exotic birds and cabbage roses, predominantly in scarlet, green and gold paint. All that was missing was the horse: the *Princess* was powered by diesel fuel, but she moved along the mysterious dark water of the canal at no more than walking pace, which was perfect for our enjoyment of the countryside we would journey through.

The interior of the narrow boat was just as nostalgic. There was the dresser, with its painted knobs, and the display of blue and white willow patterned china from the local market – probably not so cheap as it had been a century ago, but certainly just as cheerful. Cups dangled from hooks along the dresser shelves. There was a modern stove, and a shining kettle, not the black, sooty one I had fondly imagined. There was a lucky horseshoe fixed above the windows, along with polished brass ornaments. Storage was inside the bench seats, not plain hard wood as in the old days, but comfortably uphol-stered, for at nights, they doubled-up as bunks. There were more bunks in the hold, which were bagged by the young ones. The smallest room lived up to its name: you had to enter sideways on and double up under the shower. The toilet would, we were advised, need regular emptying at designated places along the route, where we could also take on fresh water.

The boat was well equipped. In the hold there were mops, brushes and buckets; life jackets; a boating hook (to fish things out of the water – hopefully not 'man overboard!') Also, a coil of rope and a can of diesel. In the dresser drawers were maps and brochures detailing places of interest. We were provided with sleeping bags with inner linings (difficult to struggle out of, when midnight visits to the loo were required.) and pillows. Lighting and cooking were by bottled gas.

We were off! The young ones untied the boat, scrambled aboard and decided to sit up top so that they could see all. John was at the wheel, and Billow lay beside him enjoying the afternoon sunshine. I was down below, unpacking the provisions we had bought in the village. A story was already unfolding in my mind, the resulting book would be called *The Summer Season*. I would set it in the past, in the heyday of the canals, I mused. I even had a name for my heroine, Ruth Owen, one of the Singing Barleys... She is a favourite heroine, to this day.

(The following sentences, which appear in my novel, were recorded the next morning, as I looked out of the window, upon waking.)

'In the clear early light of that June morning, damsel flies, tiny, translucent, blueygreen, flickered along the lush reeds below the towpath. Fish moved mysteriously, occasionally rippling the clouded waters of the canal. A cluster of ducklings, anxiously tailing duck and drake, sailed close to the narrow boat.

On the bank, wild flowers grew in sweet profusion: poppies, forget-me-nots, tall, swaying yellow flags. Below the tangled brambles, the meadow sloped away to the river. Like a painted backcloth, reminiscent of the ones before which the Barleys had so often sung, was the great mountain, brooding over all.'

The *Princess* glided smoothly along through tranquil light and shade. We marvelled at the amazing reflections of enormous trees in the water. We were experiencing life at a slower pace: we took it all in, the wild life in the fields, a flotilla of swans mirrored in the canal. We passed a boathouse which seemed to be floating on the surface of the water, a cottage or two, then a large white painted house where the turf rolled green down to the water's edge, and stone steps up to a grand entrance were flanked by mossy, sub-missively crouching statues. As we mean-dered past, the upstairs windows were flung up, one by one, the drawn curtains billowing out in the breeze. My pencil raced across the pages of my notebook. (*Ty-Gyda-Cerded*, the house with all the steps, as I later named it, was to feature in my book.)

We saw long-tailed black sheep; encoun-tered a three-legged dog, explosively defend-ing the next bridge. Billow had been sneak-ing out on to the towpath on occasion, then scrambling back aboard, but now wisely he laid doggo. The lock keeper's cottage came into view and we were about to tackle our first lock.

When I say 'we' I expect you guessed that while I was still daydreaming of coal barges lining up to go through the lock at the turn of the century, John and his young team were ready and eager to set to.

'You stay below with the dog,' John suggested kindly. 'We can manage. The lock keeper's looking out, as we're new to all this.'

I watched, bemused as Kate and Matt wound the paddles while John held the boat steady. The *Princess* rose high on the swell of water. The youngsters dashed to the far end, to operate the paddles there, so that she could float through the open gate. The crowd, mostly from the following craft, who had gathered on the bridge to watch, let out a resounding cheer.

All aboard – 'Cup of tea coming up, Mum?' was the cry. The lock keeper waved a cheery goodbye.

We went through another lock later, but although I looked forward to a repeat performance, I felt the urgent need to 'just close my eyes for a second' as we made the approach. I blamed my narrow bunk, which befitted a narrow boat, but caused fitful sleep at night. Kate said reproachfully afterwards, 'Oh, Mum, it was awful! There were even more people watching than last time, and you slept through all that rushing water, and they were peering in at you as the boat finally came up – how could you?' Very easily I'm afraid.

I also missed the unfouling of the screw when we became bogged down at Pontypool and the boatman waded in to our rescue. I awoke only as we puttered gently on our way! In the meantime, Matt and Kate had been to the local leisure centre to pass the time, and joined a class of infants in the junior swimming pool. They reported ruefully that there was a dragon of a teacher in charge who watched their every splash.

I wrote this piece of doggerel – there were

several more verses, but I'll spare you that. 'Oh we're the water boatmen; we hardly ever wash, or comb our hair, unless we're feeling posh. In my dreams I call out loud, how *can* we pass through all those locks, If we are fast asleep? While our narrow boat just rocks... Apples mixed with grubby socks...' We made quick sketches to capture the memorable moments.

Every now and then we saw a sign on the towpath. When it read, *Shop*, an arrow indicated that if we moored up, and trekked across a footpath we would eventually come to a shop, and sometimes a village, with a church and a pub, not just an isolated hamlet. There were also farms which sold eggs and milk. One morning, a farmer told us about his friend Merv the Midnight Grocer. 'We call him that, because he opens and shuts the shop when he thinks he will, and he usually delivers after dark, sometimes in the early hours. If you can catch him in the shop, you'll find he sells absolutely everything.'

We followed his directions. We had to climb a craggy wall – we heaved the old dog up between us, his leaping days were over – and when he was safely on the other side, we landed in turn with a jarring thump on the grass verge of the steep hill which we now had to climb to the village. The canals of course are low down so it is always puff-and-blow when you visit a settlement on foot.

As we reached the crest of the hill the view of the valley below was quite breathtaking. Sheep in clusters, and cottages in the dips, with purple-slated rooftops. The sun was warm on our backs, there was a further track leading up to the distant pub. Did the patrons roll downhill after closing time, we wondered? We turned left into a square, with a level path, where the shop was flanked by cottages. As the farmer had warned us, the blinds were still down. I fished in my pocket for my notebook and scribbled the following, resting the book on John's back.

'There is a cobbled courtyard before a

stable door with a hitching post for horses and a water trough. A barrel cut down for the planting of flowers and a pile of folded dusty sacks waits on the step, obviously returned by an earlier disappointed customer who failed to rouse the midnight grocer. Ivy twines through the letter box...'

(Before we even met him, I knew I would 'transport' the Midnight Grocer back in time in my story. He is Eli Pentecost in the book.)

Another customer joined us, and took up the yard broom when our knocking went unanswered. She tapped an upstairs window smartly.

The occupants of the nearby cottages opened their doors to see what was happening. The bolts shot back, the top half of the door swung open and Merv leaned his elbows on the lower half and poked his head out. He smiled at us. He had a round, jolly face and a mop of hair. 'Shop was it?' he asked sleepily. Then he beckoned us to come in, while he went behind the counter.

It really was a shop which sold literally everything and anything from sacks of potatoes, jars of sweets, mousetraps, matches and mothballs. There was not much room to manoeuvre between boxes piled on the floor. Under a glass dome on a piece of marble, on the counter, reposed a great slab of yellow saffron cake labelled 'Mother's Cake.'

I was itching to make more notes, and later on the boat, I wrote:

'Squeezed between the barley sugar sticks and blue bags of sugar was a stack of hard-crusted loaves which looked as if they would snap the consumer's teeth ... with a pencilled card: "Mother's own Bread". Along the shelves, next to jars of cloves and whole nut-megs, were pickles and jams, red, gold, green and rich brown declaring themselves to be "Mother's Gage", "Mother's Mustard Pickle", "Mother's Bramble", "Mother's Relish"...'

Now, Merv observed: 'On the boats is it? Let me take your order and I'll deliver later, wherever you are moored up for the night.'

'Er – we'll take the groceries with us now, if we may!' I said quickly.

We were all thinking his mother must be quite old but still busy with all that baking and stirring, when she appeared through the back entrance to the shop. She was not a little old lady at all, but an attractive blonde woman probably in her mid thirties. Like Merv, she had the appearance of one who had risen from her bed in a hurry.

'Meet Mother,' Merv beamed. We were none the wiser.

Mother packed our basket with her best-selling lines, a loaf of her bread, a large piece of her cake and a jar of her greengage jam. She took from the meat safe chump chops which she wrapped well in newspaper, likewise Mother's bulging, herby pork sausages.

Merv plucked the stub of pencil from behind his ear, and added to our list.

'Oh, you must try my cream cheese!' Mother told us. This looked like clotted cream in its dish. I prefer cheddar, and John, stilton, but we couldn't say no.

The best bit was yet to come. Merv didn't need a till, he had a better system. A stack of shoe boxes, labelled Pound notes, Ten bob notes, Florins, Half-crowns, Sixpences and Coppers. He took his time over sorting our change.

We said goodbye and thank you, and as we departed, the sign on the door was turned to *Closed*.

'They're going back to bed, I shouldn't wonder,' I said.

'Wouldn't you, if you'd been rowing a boat full of goods most of the night?' John replied.

'You're not supposed to travel along the canal after dark.' Matt had read all the rules.

'Precisely,' his dad said.

Our camera was constantly clicking as we journeyed on. Matt and Kate hugging the trunk of a giant tree, impossible to circle with their arms, so they peep out on either side. This tree had its roots seemingly (impossible surely?) embedded in a great rock, just as well, because it leaned alarmingly toward the water. A tall, deserted mill, with shattered windows – who had toiled there long ago? The lock cottage, now a museum, furnished simply as it had been in the past; tiny rooms. We spent some time there. We walked to the nearby river. The water here was clear and ran cold over amazing pink rocks. We all had a paddle, including Billow.

We saw a large rowing boat, with an awning, full of children wearing shorts and plimsolls, with bare brown bodies and tousled hair. They were laughing and scolding at the same time, as a couple of spaniel dogs were shaking water over the family, after an energetic dip. This family were camping on their boat and having a wonderful carefree holiday.

We came upon a film crew making a documentary for a schools' TV programme. The cameraman had obviously run out of socks like us, and we couldn't help noticing that he had the largest, filthiest feet we had ever seen, but he gave us a little talk on the rekindled interest in restoring the canals for leisure and pleasure.

We were disappointed that the tunnel was closed for repairs on this first holiday (we made up for that on later canal trips), but we pictured the leggers hanging perilously either side of the narrow boat, pushing with their feet on the slimy walls in the dark...

Another vivid memory is ascending a steep street one Sunday morning when the sun was already scorching down on us, and seeing on the front windowsill of a little terraced cottage plates of Devils-on-horseback – bacon wrapped round little sausages – and us conjecturing the reason why: a wedding feast? A party? The 'devils' wouldn't need cooking, because they were already sizzling in the heat through the glass!

This was a holiday we would never forget, and it inspired me to write full-time. *The Summer Season* was actually the fourth book I had published, because first I had a promise to fulfil in memory of my father...

Fifteen

A Writer's Companion

Now that Kate was at college, and Matt was in his last year at school, John encouraged me to write that first book. I had worn out my little portable typewriter which had succeeded the cumbersome long-carriage machine I had used for my early stories back in the orchard days, and this was replaced with my first electric typewriter. This was also a heavy machine, but needed the lightest touch, and I was used to hammering keys which often stuck together in mid-air in protest. I practiced, panicked and practiced, and gradually mastered the new technique.

It was quite a wrench to leave the village school, but the staff and pupils gave me a lovely send-off, with speeches, flowers and the latest copy of Roget's Thesaurus. I left with a bundle of thank you letters and drawings from the children. The goats were featured in one picture!

Twice a week I spent a day in the county library, researching the era I was writing about, from 1890–1920. I sat in a quiet room upstairs, with other students, and Linda, the librarian, found me all the relevant books. I wrote letters too: no internet browsing for me then! I gained several pen pals in the process, and much valuable, generously given, information. There was Dick Playle of the Music Hall Society who also knew the Isle of Sheppey well, where the first part of my novel would be set. He wrote in beautiful copperplate, and it was a pleasure to read his letters. Another new friend was Pino Maestri, the historian of London's Little Italy, who kindly sent me masses of material. I named a character in the book for him! Sheppey library provided copies of local newspaper cuttings of the time, which, written in old-style journalism, vividly brought the past to life. I also had letters my father had written about his childhood in Sheerness, his encounter with a suspected German spy, a photographer, and the terrible winter of 1895, when the sea froze, and the island had been cut off from the mainland.

It was time for us to visit the island and retrace my father's steps as he explored it with his brother and sister so long ago.

Dad was born in 1890 in 'a little cottage under the sea wall' in Sheerness. 'We opened the back door and looked over the wall at the spuming sea.' The children hardly ever wore shoes but ran barefoot over soft, clean sand – it sounded an idyllic childhood. Dad's father was in the navy and away for long periods – his mother was a wonderful cook and was steadfast in adversity. She brought her children up to be resourceful and to work hard at school. They called their mother by her Christian name, Jane, and their father was nicknamed Petty, because as Alice, my aunt said, 'He is *un petit homme* – a little man!' He was also the ship's doctor – I'm not sure he was qualified, but he was very knowledgeable and highly regarded for his skills. He had also studied Latin at grammar school.

Well, the house was still there, under the sea wall, as Dad had said. It was actually up for sale, and we did think of asking to see over it, but decided not to. Amazingly, the neighbours, when hearing the family name, had heard stories about the three mischievous children who'd lived there at the end of the nineteenth century!

We made several visits to the island, and I wrote a short story entitled *'Running with the Wind in Her Hair'* with a heroine who helped a band of smugglers in the eighteenth century. I took copious notes for the proposed novel, jottings like: 'Blue Town was so called originally because of the availability of Admiralty paint, which brightened up all the old buildings... It was 'blue' for another reason, and it was out of bounds for children and respectable folk...'

The museum was a wonderful source of material. Oil paintings of the Great Flood, the inevitable consequence of the Great Freeze after the thaw finally set in, when folk rowed boats along the main streets. Before that, water supplies had been rationed for many months! Hard times, but determined Islanders.

We walked for miles, as this was the way we could absorb the atmosphere and discover the past. *Tilly's Family* was slowly, but surely, coming together, but it would be some time yet before it was published by Piatkus. The catalyst would be the acquiring of an agent, and wise editor, Judith. She had faith in me. Thank you, Judith.

All this time, I continued writing my short stories, and receiving heart-warming feed-back from readers. Sally, my editor at the *Realm,* encouraged me with my novel research, too. I was still busy with panto-mimes and the W.I. but I missed our child-ren at home, and those at the school. June, my fruit picking friend, who was now working part-time in the local stores, asked me if I would keep Nik, her daughter, company in the school holidays, it was the perfect solution – Nik and I were already friends – she reminded me of Ginge as a small girl, dreamy and studious, always with her head in a book – like me, too, I suppose, at that age! While I encouraged Nik in her reading, and we talked about books and writing, I decided we would both benefit from going out and about, and fresh air! Nik recalls that she visited 'Sheila's old ladies' and was made a great fuss of, and shown their treasures. Nik is a true friend to this day, despite the disparity in our ages – we went to her wedding, and now she is a young mum to Izzie, she works part-time in the University library, like June, before her.

As for elderly ladies, I also volunteered to help with bathing duties at the Day Centre. Boffy had at last been persuaded of the benefits of attending the centre, after a few weeks of being collected by the special bus two mornings a week, when she disappeared after arrival while the driver was busy with wheelchairs and walking aids for the less able bodied. Boffy was off into town to do her shopping. She reappeared when it was time to go home. The staff caught up with her one day and persuaded her to go back to the centre for a bath, to have her clothes washed and then to have a hot lunch. Dear Boffy looked lovely afterwards – she chose a new outfit from a rail of clothes, her hair was soft and silvery and set in curls, and shush! she was a shade lighter... We loved her as she was, but now she was too frail to care for herself properly and too proud to ask for help.

Well, Boffy told me they needed volunteers and could she mention my name? Some of my friends were already helping with other aspects of eldercare, so why not me, I thought.

There was a special bath where the side swung out so that the one being bathed could enter easily and sit on a seat inside the bath. This 'open and close' method reminded me of the bacon slicer in the shop. As one or two of the ladies were amply built, I was always secretly worried I might unwittingly 'slice' when I closed the door... Fortunately, my fears were groundless. It was a very onerous task, and I usually got very damp. One lady, after I had been forced to change my dress for a borrowed flowery crimplene from the ever-obliging rail, looked at me and pronounced: 'You usually look so drab! You look much brighter today!'

I only ever bathed one man, and I'm afraid that was the end of my career as a bath attendant. I won't go into the reasons, but I think others had refused to bath him before me. It took ages to clean the bath...

We had reluctantly decided that we should move. We were rattling around in the chapel now – it was too big for us. We looked for somewhere nearer town and the school, a couple of miles away. We found a nice house with plenty of room for visiting family and a lovely mature garden.

'We'll be back all the time,' we promised our village friends.

But before we left, dear Boffy passed away. On Saturday afternoons, she always made her way up to the shop before it closed, to collect her regular order, two cream cakes. It was dark in the evenings now. Several people, in retrospect, mentioned that her cottage had been unlit all evening, but they had assumed Boffy was at a friend's.

Her good neighbour, Molly, raised the alarm first thing the following morning. Boffy was discovered lying unconscious in her hallway, still clutching the precious paper bag containing her treat for tea. The ambulance took her to hospital. Molly asked me what she thought Boffy would want to have to hand when she awoke. We decided, her King James bible, worn from her daily readings (she was a Christian Scientist) and a photograph of her beloved sister. Molly took them in to the hospital later, with flowers. I'm sure she knew, even if she couldn't speak. Her passing was very peaceful.

Her only relative was a distant cousin, but it was very fitting that he was an actor, we thought. When the little house was cleared, Judy and Ian bought it at auction for their mother, for it was after all, in their large garden.

Most of the village turned up to Boffy's funeral, and her cousin gave a resumé of her life. She was a fascinating character, and in my mind's eye I see her still.

It was a week before Christmas, we had just moved in to our new abode, and Sara and Phil's wedding was the following weekend! We were a full house and in happy chaos. My mother and aunt had arrived and been taken to stay with our friend Pam, who looked after them splendidly. This was after taking in John, Matt and me (and the dog) for six weeks when the chapel was sold, but we hadn't completed then on the house! Our furniture had been stored over at another friend's smallholding, as Alice had barn space. The boys coped with the moving of same from place to place!

Sara married Phil, back at the village church. She looked beautiful in an Edwardian style dress she had designed herself. This time the smallest bridesmaid wasn't Kate, but Jo's three year old Carly, our first granddaughter. We had five grandchildren now, but Di was expecting her third child, which would be another granddaughter, Hannah, in February next year.

It was a very cold day indeed, with a real threat of snow, but nothing could spoil a very happy occasion. Though I'm glad our goose pimples didn't show on the wedding photographs! Sara and Phil both love the sea, and had chosen as one of their hymns, *'For Those in Peril On The Sea.'*

They had already found their dream home, a house on a hillside, fittingly called 'Bali Hai.' This was in the Mumbles, South Wales, and they have lived there ever since. Sara has organised Sculpture On The Beach for several years, and is artist-in-residence at several local schools. Phil is a wildlife and surfing/sports photographer.

The reception was held at a local hotel and the proprietors kindly voted the wedding cake made by John and me as the best they had ever tasted! (This was before they saw the lipstick markings on a statue in the garden, and we are still wondering which of the under-fives present was responsible!)

We had our usual happy family Christmas meal around the big table. I guess the new family in the chapel were doing the same.

In the new year there was sad news of another old friend. Dear Mrs B, whom I had first met in the W.I. had died very suddenly. Meg came round to tell me. 'She was sitting at her table, with her Christmas cards spread out to choose and sign, and when I touched her shoulder, I realised she had – gone... I couldn't tell you until after the wedding and then Christmas.'

We had to carry on with the pantomime without our best singer in the wings. But we all 'felt' her presence; she was that sort of person. The W.I. put a plaque up over the kitchen hatchway in the hall, in her memory.

She was also much missed by the cricket club and the horticultural society – they present a cup at the annual show named for both Mrs B and Alf.

This is, I think, the right place to end this particular chapter in our lives. I hope you have enjoyed it – it has given me much pleasure to write about our chapel days.

I would just like to give a hint of what follows – two more marriages, in Kent, then retirement to Suffolk, where I was born, many more books written, and now, a total of 22 grandchildren, who range in age from almost two years old, to twenty-nine! Later weddings, all our family are happily settled with good partners in life, and the first of the younger generation, Hannah, will be marrying next Spring. And John and I, of course, who have already celebrated our golden wedding, are still together and enjoying new, if smaller challenges.

The publishers hope that this book has given you enjoyable reading. Large Print Books are especially designed to be as easy to see and hold as possible. If you wish a complete list of our books please ask at your local library or write directly to:

Dales Large Print Books
Magna House, Long Preston,
Skipton, North Yorkshire.
BD23 4ND

This Large Print Book, for people
who cannot read normal print,
is published under the auspices of
THE ULVERSCROFT FOUNDATION

... we hope you have enjoyed this book.
Please think for a moment about those
who have worse eyesight than you ...
and are unable to even read or enjoy
Large Print without great difficulty.

You can help them by sending a
donation, large or small, to:

**The Ulverscroft Foundation,
1, The Green, Bradgate Road,
Anstey, Leicestershire, LE7 7FU,
England.**
or request a copy of our brochure for
more details.

The Foundation will use all donations
to assist those people who are visually
impaired and need special attention
with medical research, diagnosis
and treatment.

Thank you very much for your help.